The Hippo at the End of the Hall

Helen Cooper

CANDLEWICK PRESS

This is a work of fiction. Names, characters, places, and incidents are either products of the author's imagination or, if real, are used fictitiously.

Copyright © 2017 by Helen Cooper

All rights reserved. No part of this book may be reproduced, transmitted, or stored in an information retrieval system in any form or by any means, graphic, electronic, or mechanical, including photocopying, taping, and recording, without prior written permission from the publisher.

First U.S. edition 2019
First published by David Fickling Books (Great Britain) 2017

Library of Congress Catalog Card Number 2019939256
ISBN 978-1-5362-0448-3

19 20 21 22 23 24 LBM 10 9 8 7 6 5 4 3 2 1

Printed in Melrose Park, IL, U.S.A.

This book was typeset in Adobe Jenson Pro.
The illustrations were done in pencil.

Candlewick Press
99 Dover Street
Somerville, Massachusetts 02144

visit us at www.candlewick.com

The HIPPO at the
End of the Hall

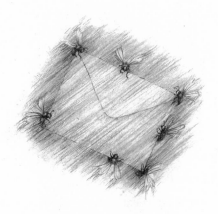

For Ian Butterworth —

for designing this book and all the others

CONTENTS

Out Of Hours

AT THE DARKEST AND MOST DESPERATE HOUR, when everyone should have been sleeping, a dull light gleamed from a pufferfish lamp in the office at the Gee Museum. The light was so dim that it hardly spilled more than shadow over the miniature printing press that stood on the desk. Yet somehow one last invitation was printed. And somehow five tiny words were added on the reverse, though these were written with a pen that was almost too large to hold. This is what the words said:

Come now or come never!

Afterward the light blinked out.

Then nothing moved until dawn, when the front doors opened just a crack, and out flew an envelope. It was addressed to 33A Treadlemill Road. It was carried off into the pewter fog by bee-mail.

1

The Invitation

CHAPTER 1

33A Treadlemill Road was a basement apartment beneath a shop on the other side of town. A boy named Ben Makepeace, who had eyes as sharp and dark as a sparrow's and tousled tawny hair, lived there with his mom. Sometimes Ben helped in the shop. Other times he helped in the apartment. That morning, when he went to bring in the milk, he found an envelope propped up behind it.

Ben was always wary of letters. Occasionally mail still came addressed to his dad, but he saw with relief that this wasn't one of those. And it wasn't addressed to his mom either. In fact, it wasn't addressed to anybody at all. The flap of the envelope was unsealed. Ben hoped it wasn't another bill. He peeked inside.

At first, seeing only a piece of thin card with a picture on it, he guessed it was an advertisement. He sneaked it out to see it better because the picture showed lots of animals. Ben liked animals — though he didn't have any pets: they weren't allowed to keep pets in that apartment. In any case, these weren't the sort of animals you could have kept at home. There was a giraffe,

3

and a hippo, and a grumpy-looking owl, and in the bottom right-hand corner was a shrewlike creature with a pendulous nose. Ben's heart began to beat faster as he gazed at the picture, for it stirred his most secret memory — a secret that he had never told to anyone at all.

"What are you doing out there?" called Mom.

Ben guiltily slipped the card back inside the envelope. Then he brought the mail to the table and laid the envelope beside it.

Mom had the same eyes as Ben but different hair, and she ran the shop upstairs. "What's that?" she said, glancing down.

"It came with the milk."

She opened the envelope, then went very still. Yet all she said, after glaring for a while, was "I thought the old Gee Museum had closed down."

Ben took the card from her and examined it as he munched his crunchy almond flakes. The shrew in the picture was holding a pen as if it had just finished writing the motto at the bottom, which read:

COME INSIDE SOMETIME.

"It looks like an invitation to get in for free," he said. "Maybe it's reopened."

"Maybe," said Mom. She was biting her lip.

"I'd like to go," said Ben.

"Would you?" Mom sounded tense.

The GEE MUSEUM

Containing the wonderful works of NATURE and Curious works of Science

ADMIT TWO Free

The Birds and Beasts will teach thee

COME INSIDE SOMETIME

"It says admit two."

"But I'm not sure when I'd have time." She looked rather pale. The rest of the mail was on the table, and as she glanced through it, Ben could tell there were a lot of bills. He knew Mom was worried about money. He knew she couldn't often leave the shop.

Their shop was called Perfect Pastimes. Once it had been simply a craft shop, but nowadays Mom sold a bit of everything: art materials and embroidery thread, buttons and yarn, stationery and stickers, and the kind of model kits that you took home and painted, and some interesting books, and

all sorts of oddments that children liked. Sometimes it was busy. More often it was not, though Mom liked Ben to help on Saturdays in case there was a rush.

Tomorrow was Saturday.

Ben waved the invitation. "Could I go myself on Sunday?"

Mom frowned at the bills and said nothing.

"You're always saying you used to go everywhere on your own at my age."

"True enough," said Mom, though her voice was unusually gruff.

"Well, then . . . can I go on my own?"

"It's . . . I don't think it's . . . Look, I like you to be independent, but it's a bit far on your own. Anyway, I don't think you'd like it."

"Where is it?" Ben turned the slip of paper over. There was no address on the back, only those five tiny handwritten words:

Come now or come never!

He peered inside the envelope and found a small brown feather nestled in the bottom — nothing else.

Mom said, "It's down by the river on the other side — close to the bridge, I think — not far from the weir, but I certainly don't want you going near *that*."

Ben sighed. "I won't go anywhere near the river. I've promised you I won't a million times. I want to go to this museum. It's not that far. Why don't you want me to go? Is there something you don't like about it?"

Mom began unpacking a box of art equipment to take upstairs. She hadn't finished her cereal. Ben was afraid she wouldn't say any more, as she so often went silent when she wanted to end a conversation. But after a moment she continued, "I never said I didn't like it. It's just . . . Anyway, since when have you been interested in museums?"

"I'm interested now. Could we have a look for it online?"

7

She chewed her lip. Then she relented. "I suppose you could have a quick look before school, seeing as you're ready. Mind you, I doubt it'll have a website — unless it's changed a lot. It used to be run by a very old lady — though she must be dead by now."

There wasn't much time. And Ben couldn't find any listing for the Gee Museum, although he found a website for the newly refurbished Discovery Museum. It looked very modern.

Mom glanced over his shoulder. "Perhaps you could go there instead," she said. "Look, it's in the center of town — that's much closer. And it's got stuffed animals too. And . . . wow, look at that lady who runs it. Do they imagine she looks welcoming?"

"She looks like a giant insect," Ben said with a giggle. "I'm not going there — she might eat me up."

"Don't be so fresh," said Mom, but she was smiling in spite of herself.

Ben didn't want to spoil her smile, so he didn't mention the museum again, but before he left for school, he propped the invitation on the shelf in his room where he kept his collection of special objects. He decided to ask his teacher about the Gee Museum. She might know something.

OPENING HOURS

DAYTIME AT THE GEE MUSEUM PASSED
AS USUAL. The building was crowded as
always — with shadows, since the windows
were small and the walls were a shade of
mahogany brown and the lights were powered
by a generator that had never worked terribly
well even when it was new. Nowadays it was not
new, and those lights shone like a flashlight
with an old battery. Sometimes they
flickered, and sometimes they went
out altogether, casting the rooms into a soft darkness that
smelled of mothballs, and honey, and long-unopened boxes,
and time passing.

All the same, the building was enchanting — if you could
get inside.

If you could get inside, you might
discover a crystal hive with live bees, or
the giant egg of an extinct elephant bird, or a
sundial that fit on a spoon.

If you could get inside, you might find a silver bottle that was rumored to contain a witch, or a fabulous and rare collection of stuffed animals, or all manner of lugubrious specimens in cabinets and drawers and jars, and some of those seemed to have a touch of magic about them.

If you could get inside — but usually you couldn't. The Gee Museum was almost always closed. Most days Constance Garner-Gee, the old, old director, felt too tired to open up for the public. Instead, she waited, hoping for something that was probably impossible, wishing, while her time and money trickled away, and the happy thoughts and words of past visitors seemed to gather in the gloom like ghosts.

A Secret and Peculiar Memory (of Dad)

CHAPTER 2

"I've never heard of the Gee Museum," said Ben's teacher. "But I've been sent a heap of information from the Discovery Museum. Would you like a leaflet for that instead?" She held one out to Ben. It had the insect woman on the front of it.

"No, thanks," he said.

She looked doubtfully at her computer screen. "Well, I can't find it online. I suppose you could try asking at the Central Library. It isn't open this afternoon, but you could ask your mom to take you tomorrow."

Ben was reluctant to mention the museum to Mom again. Anyway, she allowed him to go to the library alone. He was allowed to do lots of things alone because she was always so busy. Unfortunately Ben's friends weren't allowed the same freedom. This meant that Ben was on his own rather a lot.

Well, I like exploring on my own, he always told himself. *I'm just like my dad.*

Actually he had no real idea if this was true, because his dad was dead. He had died before Ben was three years old, had sailed away in a one-man boat and never come back.

"Lost at sea," Mom said. No one knew why or where. Mom didn't like to talk about it, and if Ben ever asked questions, she would go still and look upset, and then she would change the subject. Indeed, over the years Ben had learned there was never a good time to ask questions about Dad. He certainly couldn't ask her anything upsetting at the moment, because she was really worried about their rent. It had gone up again, and she was afraid that the landlord was planning to sell the building they lived in.

"He wants us out of here," she sometimes said. "Then he can sell the land to a developer. They make a fortune from demolishing old buildings and putting up new ones in their place."

"But it's our home," Ben always insisted when she talked this way. Mom would often look even more worried until Ben gave her a big hug and said, "We'll be all right. You'll see." And he hoped that if he said that enough times, it would be true.

Nowadays, when Ben thought of his dad, he felt curious rather than sad. The truth was that he hardly remembered him. He could recall in detail only one afternoon they had spent together, and that was a very peculiar memory. He had thought it was probably a dream — until he'd opened that envelope.

12

If it was a real memory, then he must have been very young, because he remembered Dad carrying him up some steps, through two huge black doors, and into a dark, noisy room. The noises scared him, so he buried his head inside Dad's coat. The coat lining was silky and torn. It smelled of engine oil and mint candies. It smelled good.

But Dad didn't carry him for long. After they'd crossed into the next room, Dad set him down on an expanse of dark wooden floor. A tall window cast a patch of light upon the boards. As they waited there, Ben stamped in and out of the light, feet flat and furious, because he hadn't wanted to be set down and felt rejected.

Then an old lady appeared. He could remember her blunt white hair and dark-blue dress, and her kindness.

Dad turned to Ben and beckoned him, and then they'd both followed the old lady to a doorway with a sign above it.

Through that doorway there was another doorway with a sign above it. And through that was another, and another—many repeating doorways, so that it was like standing between two mirrors and looking at the repeating reflections—except that at the very end of that long hall there stood a hippopotamus. As they'd walked along that hallway, Ben had known that the hippo was waiting for them. Yet when they'd reached it, the grown-ups had passed right by.

Only Ben held back.

All at once, with a smile that slashed its face in two, the hippo had spoken: "Life may be about to get difficult," it said with a sigh. "But you'll be safe with your mother."

Ben had resented this. He didn't always want to stay safe with Mom; sometimes he wanted to have adventures with Dad. The words confused him too. Yet he could recall them still, and as he'd grown older, they had haunted him. Even now he had such a clear picture in his mind of that gray hippo head leaning

14

down to speak to him. It had a face as cracked as the lines on a map, and eyes that winked like wise brown marbles.

After that, the memory became more fractured, like a broken jigsaw puzzle. There was another room that smelled of beeswax, with green walls and a fire. Ben remembered that as they sat down, Dad was laughing and talking, though sadly Ben couldn't picture his face.

Instead he remembered teacups: pale-green teacups decorated with china bees, and a plain blue beaker of milk for him, and he'd been glad of that because he was scared of bees — even china ones. He was even more pleased by the crusty bread that stood on the tea table. He was given a slice of it spread thickly with butter and honey. As he munched, the peppery sweet taste of it mingled with the sensible round flavor of the milk. Crumbs prickled his neck. He was rubbing at them when a shrewlike creature with a pendulous nose popped out from behind a sugar bowl. It gazed solemnly at him with eyes like small black beads.

Then it said, "It's hard to believe you'll ever be any use. At least wipe your mouth."

15

Ben did — on the back of his sleeve. When he drew his arm away, the creature was gone. The last thing he remembered was a pufferfish lantern that hung above a wooden desk. It began to glow. And then it winked at Ben. Ben tried to wink back . . .

And that was where the memory ended. He had never recalled anything more but had often wondered if someday he would be able to make more sense of it.

That evening, while Mom thought Ben was playing games on the computer, he continued his search for the Gee Museum.

For a long while he found no clues. He was about to give up for the night when he came across a link to an ancient-looking website: *The Past and Present Society Guide to Lesser-Known Museums*. It looked like no one had added anything new to the website for years, but Ben scrolled through it anyway. And with a jolt of excitement, when he had reached almost the bottom of the entries, he found what he had been looking for.

This is what he read:

THE GEE MUSEUM IN TIDBECK

DIRECTIONS

Don't bother — it's hardly ever open!
BUT if you must, there are many ways
to reach it.

BY BUS

Find the thirteenth kiosk behind the train station. From
there take the number 79 bus, which comes once a day.
Get off at the corner of Dial Avenue. The museum is
beyond the crescent, set back from the road, behind trees.

BY CAR

Unfortunately there is no parking lot. Visitors parking
without a permit have been known to be ticketed or
occasionally troubled by wild animals.

BY FOOT

The Gee Museum is a brisk fifty-minute walk from the city
center. We recommend you carry a good map.

BY STREETCAR

Probably the best way to get there.

But there aren't any streetcars, thought Ben.
He decided to go by bike.

17

Come Now or Come Never

CHAPTER 3

It was Sunday afternoon before his room was tidy and Ben was free to go.

"I'm off exploring," he said as he hugged Mom goodbye. By then he was almost itching with impatience, and nothing was going to put him off — not the cold dreary skies nor Mom's odd air of disapproval.

Even so, she lingered on the doorstep longer than usual.

"You won't go near the weir, will you?"

"I won't," Ben replied, pulling his scarf up like a spy. "I'm not stupid."

Then she insisted on fiddling with his bike.

Then she gave him a snack: some cookies in plastic wrap. He put them in his bag.

Finally, *finally*, he waved a cheery goodbye and pedaled off before she could think of any more reasons to keep him at home.

He had worked out his route the night before. Now he rode swiftly through the back

18

streets and before long reached the raw gray sweep of the river. Halfway over the bridge there was a lookout point for pedestrians and cyclists. It seemed a good place to take a break and eat those cookies while he checked the map.

He was good with maps, so much so that Mom often joked, "That boy's got a compass in his head." As far as he could tell, Dial Avenue ought to be the first road on the other side. He peered across the water, munching. On the opposite bank there was a row of old houses. Where those houses ended, a building site with half-built modern houses ran down toward the river. Beyond them he could see the edge of the weir and the disused footbridge that ran over it.

In spite of his promise, Ben would have liked to inspect the weir more closely. It looked interesting, though from the bridge, very little except the spume from the waterfall was visible. His view was blocked by a wooded peninsula of land, which projected into the river between the building site and the weir. He had a feeling the museum lay among those trees.

The leaden sky spat a fat raindrop onto his map. It spread like a hint right on the spot where he had guessed the museum would be. More rain; it was time to go if he wasn't going to get soaked. As he pedaled, he wondered again, why had Mom not wanted him to visit the museum? Was she just scared of the weir, or did she know something about that afternoon with Dad?

He had never asked her about that: partly because he had never dared, but also because it was a secret he wanted to keep to himself.

He found Dial Avenue with little trouble and biked in the rain along a row of tall, dilapidated buildings built of small black bricks. Most had several doorbells, which meant that they were apartments. None of them looked like a museum. Halfway down the road, on the side nearest the river, the dwellings ended. Perhaps a grand crescent-shaped street had once stood there, but now, behind a fence, there was a building site where stationary bulldozers and diggers rested among unfinished boxy houses. These might have made a good hideout — although something about them seemed uneasy, as if they were crouching on the surface of the riverbank wondering whether to slither in.

Beyond the mud and the tangled wasteland were the woods. Ben spotted a clock tower among those February-bare trees. He sped toward it and found a melancholy building that looked as though no one had visited it for a long time. Leaves were strewn on the driveway and had drifted onto the steps. Paint peeled from the woodwork. He pulled up at the front railing and gazed doubtfully at the dark windows and the sodden, cheese-colored facade. Was this it?

A large furry bee appeared and bumbled around his head.

Ben flapped his hands rather dramatically — he wasn't a fan of bees. Yet, once the bee had drifted toward the double doors, he called after it in a gruff deep voice that was supposed to sound confident, "What are you doing out in the rain?"

The bee didn't reply — not that Ben had expected it to — but it landed on a small sign to the left of the doors. Ben got off his bike and ran up the steps to read it. This is what it said:

THE GEE MUSEUM
········· OPEN: ·········
Every third Monday 2:00–4:00 p.m.
Every fourth Wednesday 1:00–3:00 p.m.
Every second Saturday 2:00–4:00 p.m.

THE REST OF THE TIME CLOSED.

So he *had* found it.

But it wasn't open on Sundays.

And even if tomorrow was a third Monday, there wouldn't be time to come after school. He'd have to hope Mom would let him come the following Saturday — if next Saturday was a second Saturday. How could he even know?

Confused, he trudged back down the steps. The rain was turning torrential. And he was cold and deeply disappointed. And though he tried to be brave, the sides of his mouth kept dragging downward as if little weights were pulling at their corners. In fact, he felt as miserable as the sobbing sky.

Across the road a café leaked light onto the flooding pavement. Above the steamed-up windows was a very welcoming sign with an image of a cake.

Ben knew it wasn't safe to ride home in this sort of rain. He fumbled in his bag. At the bottom he found a few coins stuck to a fluffy hard candy. Maybe he had enough for a muffin? He locked his bike to the railing, then crossed to the café.

Inside, the café was warm and smelled of wet coats and coffee and freshly baked cake. Other damp customers were drinking and eating. Ben gazed like a hungry dog at the cakes beneath the glass. There were no price labels.

"How much is a slice of that?" he asked, pointing to a honey-colored sponge cake topped with cherries.

The waitress named more money than he had.

Ben lost his nerve and pointed to a carton of orange juice he knew he could afford. "I'll have that instead."

"To drink in here?" the waitress said, curling her lip as she picked up the sticky coins.

23

Ben nodded glumly.

"I'll bring it to your table."

He slunk to a booth near the window so that he would know when the rain died down. Presently his unwanted juice arrived with an unwanted glass. The waitress turned with her tray and unloaded coffee and a hunk of oozing chocolate cake at the booth opposite, where a thick-necked man in an over-tight coat had his nose buried in some papers. Ben's eyes tracked the cake. The man was a clumsy eater. Crumbs spilled down his front as he munched. His thick lips looked almost too big for his mouth, and his teeth were pointed and crowded as if he possessed more than the usual number.

The door opened, creating a draft.

The man rose with chocolate frosting smeared on his chin and waved to the woman who entered. The woman was tall and thin and beige, from her pointy shoes to the top of her smooth, round head. Even her umbrella was beige. Her large crocodile handbag was beige; her cat's-eye glasses were beige; her smile was beige; everything was beige, except her nails, which were painted a nasty shade of purple. And Ben recognized her. She was the director of that new Discovery Museum — he'd seen her picture on its website. He decided that in real life she looked even more like a tall, sinuous insect.

Her protruding eyes darted nervously around the café. "You're sure it's wise to talk now?" she murmured.

"Don't worry," the man said, waving her to his table. "It's very private here." He paused to wink. "Glad you could make it early. I'd like to go over a couple of things before we head across the street to the old lady. I didn't want to use the phone. You never know . . ."

". . . who's listening in?" the woman finished for him.

The man nodded.

Ben was curious. *Mom mentioned an old lady at the museum,* he thought. And he pricked up his ears.

Eavesdropping

CHAPTER 4

A plate of the honey-colored cherry cake arrived for the insect woman. She took a polite bite, then left it while she pulled a folder from her bag. Ben could smell the cake.

The woman said, "How an old lady runs a museum on her own, I can't imagine. Are you sure you've never seen any other staff?"

The man slurped his coffee. "Never," he said. "No idea how she does it; she must be ancient."

The woman squeezed lemon into her tea. "She does seem to have been there forever — I've looked into it very carefully — and there really doesn't seem to be anyone waiting to take over after she goes. The museum's always belonged to the Gee family, and she's the last of them. There's no record of any surviving heirs."

The man nodded. "Actually there was a relative, a cousin of some sort, but he drowned several years ago. And for some reason there are no trustees either. In fact, there's no evidence that anyone else is interested in the place — it's a ridiculous way to run a museum."

The insect woman picked up her cake as if to take a bite but returned it to the plate untasted. "Surely she'll sell?" she said. "It must be such a struggle to keep the place open at her age."

"It's hardly ever open."

"Do you think the city council will step in and save it?"

"They might have, but you know yourself they haven't had any funds since the flood last year. Any extra cash for this area would go to fixing up the weir. It's a mess — could even be dangerous."

"Well, she can't go on running a museum forever."

"You'd think not," said the man with a bitter laugh, "but I've been trying to get her to sell me the place for years. I could build a lot of houses on that land."

So that's it, thought Ben in disgust. *He's a property developer, maybe like the one who wants to buy Mom's shop.*

"Well, hopefully, we'll persuade her to sell," said the woman. Her pale thin tongue flicked briefly over her top lip. "But what's your plan if she still refuses?"

And with those words, their conversation changed. They began to speak lower. Their heads drew closer, and the looks that passed between them grew secret and unpleasant.

"I don't have much time left," hissed the woman, clasping her hands. Two purple talons rested under her pointed chin. "The funding will go elsewhere if I don't move fast. Have you thought of some way to . . . well . . . to *persuade* the old lady that she needs to sell quickly?"

The man was very still.

She leaned forward. "The museum's in a terrible state. I'd've thought a little bad luck — like . . . maybe an infestation of vermin — might close her down for good."

The man rubbed his nose. "You talking rats? Or insects?"

"Well . . . something along those lines." She glanced at the cake and then slipped her hands into the opposite sleeves of her jacket. (Ben thought this made her look like a praying mantis.)

"A flood would finish things faster," the man grunted.

"But that could damage the exhibits." The woman pursed her neat little mouth. "Unless, of course, it were only a small flood . . . The best of the collection is well above ground level. A small flood might be safe enough. It would ruin the building, though . . . wouldn't it? Mold and rot, filth from the river, overflowing sewers — the cleanup would be expensive, don't you think?"

"Bound to be," the man said with a smirk. "Old buildings like that cost a pile to fix up — and flooding is a possibility this winter. That weir's not been maintained properly. I've been keeping an eye on it because we're still working on the land next door."

"I realize that." The woman withdrew one hand from her sleeve, and two purple nails tap-tap-tap-tapped on the table the way a spider might tap on a web. "So . . . you think a flood might be . . . arranged?"

The man rubbed his stumpy neck thoughtfully. "Accidents do happen. . . . Burst water main, maybe . . . ? Or at this time of year, with the river this high, if something fell into the weir and blocked it . . . that might cause a lot of trouble."

There was a heavy pause.

"Might it?" Her pale eyes stared fixedly.

The man sniffed.

She regarded him with a predatory gaze. "I have to have it."

The man gave one sharp nod. "I understand."

Now the woman leaned back. "Well," she said briskly, "with luck that won't be necessary. I have a very enticing proposal for her here." She passed the folder to the man. "I think we're worrying about nothing. At her age I suspect it would be a huge relief to sell. She could retire very comfortably on what we're offering."

"And who could resist you?" The man's jowls wobbled into a sharky smile. "If anyone can charm the old lady, you can."

The woman laughed like a cracking mirror. "You're very confident."

"I am now that you're on board. And I've got friends who can push this through once she's signed on the line."

"I'll bet you have."

He paused to look at his flashy watch. "Look, we're not due there for another twenty-five minutes. Time for another cup while I have a last look through the corrections . . . and you haven't eaten your cake. Do you mind if I . . . ?"

"Go ahead," she said, pushing her plate toward him.

Ben's heart thudded. These people were planning to flood the museum — on purpose!

He had to tell someone.

But who should he tell?

The police?

Would they believe him?

Would they believe a boy instead of this important-seeming beige insect lady? He knew that they wouldn't. They would say he hadn't understood what he'd heard. Or they'd say he shouldn't eavesdrop on grown-ups.

So would Mom.

There was only one thing he could do. He must warn the old lady himself.

The waitress reappeared. Ben slipped out behind her broad back, hoping he wouldn't be noticed. The insect woman glanced up sharply as he left.

"It's just a kid," Ben heard the man say.

Time and Feathers

CHAPTER 5

Ben splashed back up the museum steps and knocked on the great wooden doors. Then he glanced over his shoulder, half expecting to see the insect woman watching him through the café window.

She wasn't watching.

But nobody answered the door.

He knocked again, more urgently this time.

The doors remained shut, solid and forbidding, and he saw that the lintel was festooned with cobwebs as if the doorway had been undisturbed for a while.

Or else they were spun by tropical super-spiders, he worried. Ben didn't like insects. He especially didn't like insects that stung, yet here came another of those bees that shouldn't have been out in February at all. The bee flew over his head and bumped against the crack between the doors.

Another bee joined it.

Then a third.

This was too many bees for Ben. When he turned, he saw more bees dancing in the rain above the steps behind him. The bees at the door flew to join them. They seemed unusually dark and fat. They seemed to be blocking his way — or that is what he thought as he retreated in panic until his back was pressed hard against the doors, and when he couldn't go any farther backward, he begged the building desperately, "*Please* let me in!"

He didn't really expect the doors to open. But all of a sudden they swung inward. He was leaning so hard against them that he stumbled and almost fell. Then, while he was catching his balance, the door slammed:

BANG!

And Ben had a sense of leaving the world behind.

He was in a dark lobby, surrounded by the mechanical creaking and ticking of an orchestra of clocks of every shape and size.

Who had let him in?

He saw nobody, yet the back of his neck prickled, and he had a sense of something that might have been green — if there had been light to see it by — something small, that scuttled down the door and fled across the flagstones.

And gradually, as he grew accustomed to the dark, he saw that in addition to the clockfaces that lined the walls, there were eyes gleaming back at him.

They were the tawny eyes of hawks, the red eyes of waterfowl, the smaller bead-black eyes of songbirds. Perched on top of each clock was a bird, and all those birds faced the door, and what with the eyes, and the clockfaces, and the flagstones, and the faraway shadowy ceiling, Ben felt as if he had interrupted a private church ceremony.

"They're only stuffed birds," he told himself.

His voice in that stone room sounded louder than he had meant it to. A small owl that was perched on top of an elaborate casement clock appeared to stare down at him with disapproval — in fact, if a glare could be loud, this owl's glare would have been deafening.

Ignore it, thought Ben. *It's only a stuffed owl.*

He turned from the owl to face a wicked-looking shoebill that stood before the empty ticket booth. The booth was unlit, unoccupied. Beyond it, the museum curved to the right. All that was visible immediately ahead was an oil painting of a family group in old-fashioned clothes. The grown-ups in the painting looked rather somber, but there was a girl with tawny hair who sat in the center, wearing the sort of secret smile that could brighten any room. That smile seemed to welcome him in. Encouraged, he took a couple of steps. That was when he felt an odd tingle through his shoe and immediately the casement clock with the owl on top began to chime.

Ben jumped.

The clock struck the hour seven times. Yet the hands on the painted face indicated that it was 3:55. The clock shouldn't have been striking at all.

It's an old clock, Ben said to calm himself. *There's just something wrong with it.*

Then it occurred to him that the chime and the buzz he had felt in his foot had seemed instantaneous. Could the chime be a signal, like a doorbell announcing his presence?

This seemed unlikely. Yet when he raised his foot, he saw a flat brass button embedded in the flagstone. He figured that standing on this button might make the clock chime. It seemed foolish to test this theory by stepping on the button again. Yet he did it anyway. And the clock repeated its chime.

Silver echoes floated through the building.

"Now someone will come," he muttered.

He remembered the invitation and tugged it from his pocket. This time he noticed that the owl in the picture was not unlike the one on the casement clock. He looked back at the real owl. He had a feeling that it had moved — its head looked straighter.

"Don't be silly," he told himself, and strode over to examine the painting. He wanted to look at the girl instead of the scowling owl.

As he drew closer, he saw that the picture was full of animals too. He noticed that one of the young men had a chameleon on his shoulder, and even a stern old lady had a mouse in her pocket — or it could perhaps have been a shrew, like the one on the ticket; it was hard to tell. Ben wondered how it would feel to be part of a big family with so many animals.

"Lucky," he murmured wistfully. "I wonder who they were."

A brass plaque on the wall below held the answer. It was engraved with these words:

THE GARNER-GEE FAMILY C. 1889
We welcome all who visit our collection.

"Well, I'm a visitor," announced Ben, "and I've got an invitation."

One of the other young men in the painting had an owl perched behind him. It looked rather like that same owl again. Ben turned to the real owl and flapped his invitation at it. The gesture felt foolish even as he did it, so he hurried to the adjoining room, glad that no one had seen him.

The Other End of the Hall

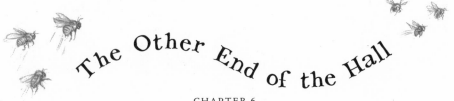

CHAPTER 6

Next door, the wall held glass cabinets full of more birds. Most were posed among faded models of their natural habitats. Some were hunting. Some were nesting. Some were eating. All of them seemed watchful.

In the center of the room was a long cabinet that ran from the wall on Ben's left across the room and most of the way to the window. Nowadays it is illegal to collect birds' eggs, but in the nineteenth century it was quite respectable. Since the Gee Museum dated from the Victorian era, it had a substantial egg collection, which was displayed in this cabinet. The smallest egg, to the left, was the pea-size egg of a hummingbird. Other eggs were arranged by size, until at the far end, near the window, you reached the largest of all: the rare egg of the extinct elephant bird. It was bigger than a football and had a label, which announced that the shell was large enough to hold the contents of 180 chicken eggs.

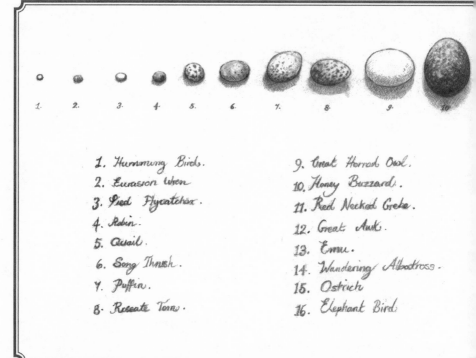

1. Humming Birds.
2. Eurasian Wren
3. Pied Flycatcher.
4. Robin.
5. Quail.
6. Song Thrush.
7. Puffin.
8. Roseate Tern.
9. Great Horned Owl.
10. Honey Buzzard.
11. Red Necked Grebe.
12. Great Auk.
13. Emu.
14. Wandering Albatross.
15. Ostrich
16. Elephant Bird

Normally Ben would have been fascinated. Not today. Now, as he strode along the length of that cabinet, he was seeking something beyond it, feeling as alert as a wild bird himself, using not only his eyes and ears but also some extra, wilder sense that drew his feet — *squeak, tap, squeak, tap* — over wide, dark floorboards until he reached the end of the room, where, below a long window, a bright patch of sky was reflected on the wooden surface.

When Ben rounded the corner of the cabinet, he could see

ELEPHANT BIRD.
Aepyornis maximus. Extinct.
Loc. Madagascar

EURASION WREN.
Troglodytes troglodytes.
Loc. Sussex 1863
F.G.G 1872.

the wall that had been obscured. And he halted in that patch of light. Then, fizzing with recognition, he punched the air with his fist.

Because this was the place he had visited with his dad.

Because it had been no dream.

Because right in front of him was a doorway with an exit sign above it, which led to a long, narrow hall. And waiting at the end of it was a hippopotamus.

From out of the hallway, Ben heard quiet music echoing, as

if it flooded from a faraway open space like a swimming pool. He even recognized the tune, having heard it at school: it was the "Aquarium" music from *The Carnival of the Animals*. The weirdness of hearing music playing in a museum almost caused him to forget the couple in the café. He forgot about tiptoeing and paced into the hall, ignoring open doorways to the left and right. He passed a silver ship, a room full of fossils, another of insects, and one filled with bottles; he passed rooms displaying a multitude of treasures, and all the while the pipes that lined the length of the ceiling seemed to gurgle in encouragement. Yet, as he strode closer, the hippo began to appear smaller than he had imagined it would be. This made him hesitate. Then, when he emerged from the hallway, he momentarily stopped altogether. Most people did when they entered the central atrium of the Gee Museum.

The hippo stood on a wooden podium, four steps down, in a sunken courtyard. It was bathed in an opalescent light that spilled from the high glass ceiling. Beside it, on a taller plinth, stood a windup gramophone. The music poured from the gramophone's horn, which ought to have seemed very strange, but Ben was so excited that he hardly noticed. Instead he was struck to discover what you couldn't see until you reached this position: the hippo was surrounded by a huge and wonderful menagerie of other animals.

Near the hippo was a group of baboons, and a sitting polar bear, and a walrus, and a russet kangaroo (which was larger than expected), and a huge moose with antlers like the branches of an oak, and an anteater, and a family of collared peccaries (a sort of wild pig), and there was a black panther, and a golden lioness lying with her cub, and a tawny camel on a patch of sand it shared with a chocolate-colored llama that looked like its child but wasn't, and Ben could see the brindled shell of a giant turtle, and the curled-up armor of an armadillo, and the white stripes of zebra and okapi, and the jigsaw-puzzle coats of giraffes. There were nine giraffes, though not all of them were whole; some were only displayed as far as their heads or necks, and only two were complete. These stood to one side of the steps that led

up to a gallery level. On the other side of
the stairs, there was a small dinosaur
skeleton.

Upstairs, among more glass cabinets,
he could see there was
an empty wooden
chair. It had a red
cushion that had been pushed to one side, as if somebody had
been sitting there recently. But Ben couldn't see anyone around
now. After a moment, he tiptoed down the four steps into the
sunken courtyard and stood beside the hippo.

45

He hesitated then, unsure what to do. It was the same hippo, all right: the same shiny mud-gray hide, the same cracked face, the same smell of mothballs and honey. Close up, it was indeed a smaller animal than it had seemed when viewed from the confines of the hall. It was hardly bigger than a Shetland pony. But that was because it wasn't an ordinary hippopotamus at all: it was a pygmy hippo, which is an altogether different species of animal. Yet despite its small size, it still had great dignity, and a haunting air of importance that made it seem more present than anything else in the room. Ben felt safe standing beside it. He was reluctant to move anywhere else, though the skeptical, mature part of him knew he must have imagined it talking to him in the past.

What am I hoping for? he wondered.

The wistful part of him that wasn't so eager to grow up wished very hard that the hippo would speak. Because if it could, maybe it would tell him something, just anything, about his dad.

Abruptly the gramophone needle reached the end of the record and played a repeated crackle.

Crackle bump!

Crackle bump!

Ben looked at it. Who had set the record turning?

Crackle bump!

46

Seven, eight, nine cycles of the needle. *Crackle bump!*

The sound pressed on him, like a trap slowly cranking shut.

Ten, eleven times.

Crackle bump,

crackle bump . . .

All at once a clock chime rattled through the gramophone horn!

It chimed seven chimes!

It was the chime from the clock in the lobby, yet the sound of it was broadcasting straight through the speaker horn.

So, he had guessed correctly: the casement clock did function as an alarm.

Abruptly the gramophone horn began broadcasting other sounds from the lobby. Ben remembered the brass button he'd stepped on. He guessed it must work like one of those monitors people use to hear a sleeping baby in another room.

This is what he heard through that monitor horn: footsteps on the flagstones, the front doors slamming shut, then two voices speaking from the lobby — a man and a woman.

It was the couple from the café.

They've walked in without knocking, he thought.

In a horrible rush he realized that the front doors must have been left unlocked, ready for them to make their way inside.

"They were invited!" he moaned out loud. "I'm the trespasser."

47

It got worse. He could hear them through the speaker horn, and this is what they said:

"Look, it's only a child's bike. Could be anyone's," the man declared.

"It could be," the woman said. "But I still think that boy was listening to us. I bet it's his bike out there."

"So what if it is his bike?" said the man. "A boy that age wouldn't have understood. Probably just drooling over the cake you weren't eating. I haven't seen him before, and I'm a regular. The waitress had never seen him either — she said so."

"All the same . . ."

"Well, even if he did hear us, what's a kid going to do? We're making a totally legit offer for the building and the collection. Nothing wrong with that. Should suit everyone. And this time the old lady must be interested — she's invited us for tea, hasn't she? Can't imagine she'll let some kid put her off the whole deal."

"You're right," fluttered the woman's voice. "Sorry to be jittery. Those bees outside made me nervous — I'm sure they shouldn't be there at this time of year. And there's so much at stake. Some of these clocks are fabulous."

"Worth the effort, isn't it? Think what you could do with them."

"If I had the room."

"Well, you will have the room when I've built it. Think about the nice new extension I'm going to build on to the Discovery Museum — and forget the kid. He's not important."

"He couldn't already be with the old lady?"

"Don't be paranoid. The doors were shut, weren't they? The old lady said to come right in and she'd meet us upstairs, so she's not likely to have met the kid at the door. If by any tiny chance he got inside in the last five minutes, he'll be close by."

"And if he is?"

The man grunted. "Then I'll deal with him."

The Sengi

CHAPTER 7

Hide till they've gone! Ben told himself.

Where?

Behind him a large ebony cabinet displayed small mammals on glass shelves against a map of Africa. It didn't run the whole length of the wall; there was a small gap at one end between the cabinet and a corner of the building. He dashed for that gap. The upper half of the cabinet was glass, so he had to wedge himself in backward, hunkering down below the glass-line, to be sure of being hidden. He was very cramped.

Tock, tock, tock: the woman's pointed heels clacked on wood, so they must have reached the egg room. The footsteps paused.

Was she searching for him?

Ben imagined her pointed face goggling into every corner. Was this hiding place good enough? He wasn't sure, yet he didn't dare look for somewhere better. All he could do was take deep ragged breaths to calm his hammering heart. Unfortunately the corner was as dusty and grimy as a vacuum bag, so the deep breathing made him feel sneezy. *He couldn't sneeze now!*

51

Desperately he nipped the bridge of his nose. That didn't work: his nose and eyes throbbed with the itch. He wriggled his nose; he made wild anti-sneeze faces; all his attention was bent on not sneezing, and none of his attention was focused on the creatures in the cabinet.

Whereupon the nearest one made a face back at him!

Ben's sneeze vanished, shocked clean away, because he saw — right beside him on the other side of the glass — the shrew from the long-ago tea table.

He stared. The creature was motionless. *Did I imagine it moving?* he thought.

He examined the label beside it:

SENGI — MACROSCELIDES PROBOSCIDEUS
Also known as the short-eared elephant shrew. Female.
Capt. F. Garner-Gee: Southern Africa, 1869

This sengi was so obviously stuffed, tatty, battered at the edges — he could even see the seams. The bead-black eyes gazed ahead, glassy.

"You didn't move," Ben whispered firmly, trying to convince himself.

As he said that, she leaped, rearing up so that her hairy face and tiny brown-pink paws pressed on the glass, alarmingly close to his nose.

Ben jerked, bashing his head on the wall. "Ow!"

"SHHH!" scolded the tiny creature. She had a shrill, high voice, clear as a squeaky cat toy, even from behind the glass. "And don't you dare back away. You stay and listen — seeing as you can hear me."

"I . . . I'm not going anywhere," said Ben shakily.

"You'd better not. *How* you'll get out of this fix, I can't imagine. Trapped now, aren't you? So hush up or they'll hear you."

And Ben, who was astonished beyond measure, discovered that he had reached a state of mind where nothing was too astonishing to believe and found himself talking back to the shrew. "Maybe *you* should hush. They might hear *you.*"

"Grown-ups only hear what they expect to hear," said the sengi. "That rarely includes me."

"They might expect to hear me," said Ben.

"Well, then, *you'd better be quiet!*" The shrew grabbed her tail and gnawed at it.

But Ben was unable to be silent now. "You've got to watch those people," he whispered. "I overheard them planning something really bad. I need to tell the old lady who runs the museum about it. If she's here."

"She's here all right, but you'd better stay hidden."

This was only too obvious. Ben could hear the couple coming down the hall. *Tock, tock, tock* went the lady-sharp heels, followed by another pause. He guessed they were searching for him in one of the side rooms.

"What *did* you overhear?" asked the sengi, wriggling her long nose restlessly. (She could gyrate that nose in a circle, almost as cleverly as an elephant can gyrate its trunk.)

"That man said he wanted to buy the museum so that he can knock it down and build new —"

"We know *that*," spat the shrew. Her tail shot out of her mouth and shook like an angry question mark. "Julian Pike's been sniffing around here for years. Our director has always told him *No sale!*"

"A . . . you mean your human director? D'you mean the old lady?"

"Her *name* is Constance Garner-Gee, and she's more than a director. She's the curator of this museum too, and the owner, and chief label-writer, and cleaner and duster, and never in all these years has she ever, ever, *ever* agreed to talk to one of those building-smasher people. But it's different now that Miss Tara Snow's involved."

"Tara Snow?"

"That woman out there."

"She runs the Discovery Museum," said Ben. "She isn't very nice either."

"She's the civilized face of destruction," declared the shrew.

"I . . . suppose you could say that," said Ben. He was peering beyond the shrew to the hall entrance, dreading the couple's appearance. Yet the shrew was scuttling back and forth, trembling with agitation. What if they noticed her moving when they came into the room? They easily might if she carried on like this. And then they might spot him too.

"I do say that," said the shrew. "Tara Snow has decided that there's only room for one museum in this town — hers — and she wants to pinch the best bits from the Gee collection and put them in her museum and then let Julian Pike smash up our lovely home."

"You mean she wants to steal the things in here?"

"Not exactly. She'll pay money. Not enough, but that's not the point. The point is, this museum is our home and she wants to move us . . . But not all of us . . . Don't you understand?

She doesn't want the whole collection in her modern museum. We've heard she's only interested in what she calls 'the choicest exhibits,' and on a rotating basis. Do you know what that means?"

Ben shook his head.

"It means some of us will be put in *storage*! Piled in her moldy basement, rotting in the dust where no one can see us and our spirits will shrivel . . . and that'll be the fate of the luckier ones." The sengi paused to stuff both paws and tail into her mouth.

"What will happen to the unlucky ones?"

"Humans call it *recycling*," the shrew said indistinctly. "There won't be enough storage room for everyone, so some will be sold . . . but most will be sorted into plastic bins and . . ." She stopped then and scrabbled in a circle before squeaking, "We'll be squished into something else, or burned in a furnace, or thrown in the trash to rot, and no one will care *at all*."

"I care," Ben said. "Can't someone do something to stop them?"

"We've already done something. We've found you."

"*You* found *me*?" Ben's jaw dropped. "What d'you mean? I'm here because a free invitation came with the mail."

But the shrew's whiskers were quivering fiercely. "Who do you think delivered that envelope?" she jabbered. "It wasn't the mailman. Do you have any idea how hard it was for us to print that ticket? Leon and I struggled for hours with the printing machine. Before that, the bees lost several days of honey production hunting you down, and not a few more were waterlogged carrying that heavy paper in the fog. Then what do you do? You repay our hard work by sauntering in TOO LATE!"

"I came as soon as I could," Ben said.

"Well, it wasn't soon enough," snapped the shrew. "And if you can't think of some clever way to stop them, then our only hope is that Constance will send them away."

"Why don't you talk to her yourself?"

"Because she can't hear any of us. She hasn't heard us since she was about your age. Not that it mattered much — she's always had a feeling for us and she loves this museum. But nowadays she seems so tired. And old. And we're worried about her — she's talking to herself much more than she used to. Mind you, that has its uses because we have an idea of what's going on from what she says . . . but it seems to us she's run out of reasons for living."

There was a suspicious wateriness around the sengi's eyes.

She looked so vulnerable and sad that Ben put out a finger and stroked the glass, whereupon she shuddered from her bristling head to the tip of her tail and bared needlelike teeth as she squeaked, "Don't you *dare* treat me like a toy."

"Shhhhh," Ben said, wincing.

"Yes, hush!" said a coppery voice from somewhere in the center of the courtyard. "They're almost upon us."

Measuring Time

CHAPTER 8

Julian Pike and Tara Snow emerged from the hallway.

"You see?" said Pike. "No sign of any boy."

"He could be hiding," said Tara Snow.

Pike shrugged. "Well, I can't see him. Can you?" He strutted down the four steps like he owned the place already. "What do you make of this lot?"

Tara Snow surveyed the animals with disdain. "There's far too much taxidermy," she declared. "Though there are a few very fine exhibits I'd be interested in keeping."

"What's taxidermy?" whispered Ben to the sengi.

"Us," she replied. "I suppose *you* would say stuffed animals."

The woman pointed at the hippo. "That one's no good. It's split at the seams. No use to me like that. Anyway, stuffed animals aren't so popular these days—times have changed since the Victorians went out hunting and collecting. I'm only interested in displaying a few of the more unusual examples. The rest can be scrapped."

Pike winced, raising his eyebrows meaningfully to the ceiling. "Scrapped? Don't forget, the old lady's hoping to keep all the collection together. She mentioned *scientific importance.*"

"I expect some of it *is* scientifically important," said Tara Snow. "But that's the best I can offer."

"Well, I wouldn't mention that till the deal's done," said Pike.

They crossed the floor. The woman continued to make expansive gestures, but soon Ben couldn't hear her words. He worried that the sengi would resume her scampering. She was gnawing her tail so savagely that he feared she might chew it off altogether. Suddenly she reared up and gestured upstairs. "Here comes Constance."

Ben saw that a door on the gallery level had opened. A lady with short white hair and a long dark dress stepped through it. Although she was old and walked with a cane, she was stately: she stalked along the length of the gallery like a hunting heron, chin up, face set and determined. When she reached the top of the staircase, Ben was certain she was the old lady from his memory, because as she spoke, he recognized her voice. It was sweet and dark as licorice.

"Welcome" was all she said at first. But the couple downstairs had been too engrossed in themselves to be aware of her presence. So they jumped.

Ben suspected Constance Garner-Gee had meant to startle them and had enjoyed it. (If he hadn't been so frightened, he might have enjoyed it himself.)

"Do come on up," she added with a frosty smile. "I have tea ready in the office . . . although — as I told you before — I am not sure your ideas will make sense for me. You must understand, this is my family home as well as a family museum."

"Ohhhhh . . . I do understand," gushed Tara Snow, darting eagerly toward the stairs. "Such a super collection. I'm only here because I'm *sooo* interested in its future."

"Suffering centipedes," said the sengi, quivering with horror. "Constance is *interested* in what they have to say. Look, she's encouraging them."

"Well, it won't help if she tells them she's not selling," whispered Ben as the couple climbed the steps to the gallery.

"What d'you mean?"

"I didn't finish telling you." Ben began to recount what he'd heard in the café. But as soon as he mentioned a flood, the sengi became so agitated that she foamed at the mouth.

"They're going to flood the museum!" she hissed. "And you've been *wasting time* — you great galoot!"

"I haven't . . . I — I did try to tell you —"

"Shhhh, while I think what to do," snapped the sengi. "This means we have even less time than we thought!" She grabbed her tail again and bit it nervously as they watched the grown-ups strolling the length of the gallery upstairs.

Tara Snow simpered at Constance, "Such a pity so few people see this. You're not open very often, are you? Such a shame. Oh, I know you still need to be convinced — but I'm sure we can come to an agreement: we intend to exhibit the

Gee collection in a beautiful purpose-built annex. Imagine! People would be able to see some of these wonderful objects every day — instead of only now and then."

"We're talking quality building for the new annex," added Julian Pike. He indicated the cracks in the ceiling and the rotten window frames with a wave of his stubby hand. "I want to build a new clean space for the Discovery Museum that the city will be proud of — and it will be named after your family, don't forget."

"Yes, we'll call it the Gee wing," said Tara Snow, with her head cocked coyly to one side.

"And you'll display all of it?" said Constance Garner-Gee. "This is a huge collection."

"Oh, we will rotate the exhibits," Tara Snow said smoothly. "At any one time you'll see a portion of it properly curated with superb lighting and spacious modern cases."

"And you'll have room to store the rest?"

But Tara Snow dodged that question. Instead she spoke of interactive labeling while she smiled like a poisoner and ran her predatory purple nails along the cabinets of scientific instruments, and she asked lots of questions in her brittle polyester voice about the telescopes and the microscopes and the astrolabes and sundials,

and she asked about the devices for drawing maps, and the devices for measuring snowflakes, or electric static, or for measuring no one knew what anymore, and her eyes brimmed with such hypnotic fascination that soon Constance Garner-Gee began to look more convinced. Together the two women entered the office looking more relaxed.

Behind them Julian Pike smirked. He paused as they went inside and examined the courtyard below, leaning forward, his eyes narrowed, pudgy hands gripping the balustrade. His square head moved slowly. Scanning.

In his corner Ben folded himself tighter than he'd thought possible.

As Julian Pike sniffed and rubbed his bulky nose, a bee landed on the banister beside his hand. He watched it for a moment. Then he brought the side of his fist down square upon it: *BANG*. He brushed away the remains of the bee with a nasty smile, as if he had enjoyed killing it. After that he

nodded in a satisfied way, then he followed the women into the office. Behind him the door clicked shut.

Immediately the sengi began to scrabble in a circle. "Hell's bells and buckets of camel dung, Constance was enjoying talking to that woman," she said breathlessly. "I know she was, oh she was, she was, didn't you think so? *Enjoying it!* That woman's going to persuade her to sell. I'll have to find a way to warn her she's being tricked . . . though I'm not sure how. Oh, you stupid boy, you've bungled everything. If only you'd come in time to warn her yourself."

"I came as soon as I could," protested Ben, scrambling onto his feet, which were so numb they didn't feel like they belonged to him. "Why are you blaming me?" he cried. "What's it got to do with me?"

The shrew's nose gyrated wildly. "It's got *everything* to do with you. Don't you understand? Your future as well as ours depends upon this."

Then, before he could say another word, she whisked across the shelf and scrambled through a hole at the back of the cabinet. A moment later, she reappeared at ground level and scooted for the stairs, bounding up the steps on both back feet like a tiny kangaroo.

Ben tried to follow, but his cramped legs wouldn't move quickly enough. He was left among the menagerie of wild animals in the sunken courtyard. He knew that another of them had spoken to him. But they were all as still as the cast-iron pillars that held up the roof. Perhaps they could move if they chose? He could see that most of them had a lot of teeth....

He wished he was back home with Mom.

The Hippo

CHAPTER 9

Ben knew that with wild animals you aren't supposed to make eye contact or any sudden movements; you just move very, very slowly away. He slunk toward the exit with slightly bent knees, like a jungle explorer he had seen on TV. He slid past the lions and a zebra, past the polar bear and the wild pigs. None of them stirred. Now only the hippo stood in the way. As he crept by, he couldn't resist sparing it a glance.

Once again he felt unsettled by the hippo's small size, for when he hadn't been looking squarely at it, he'd had the impression of a huge presence. It was as though the essence of the hippo filled more space than its body did.

The hippo's eyes twinkled back. They looked amused.

Ben hesitated.

Then there was no doubting it: the lines deepened around the hippo's eyes, and its mouth broadened to a smile as wide as a boulevard.

When it spoke, it had a voice as soft as suede: "Welcome, Ben."

That was all it said, though Ben saw its teeth — they were yellowish, cracked, and wild.

His reply came out in a nervous croak: "Hello."

It didn't matter; the hippo continued now that it had begun: "It's good to see you, Ben. This is such a special day for us."

"Is it?" mumbled Ben. He was finding the hippo a little alarming. He was nervous about the lions too. (He had remembered that the sengi had mentioned someone called Leon. Wasn't that the sort of name a lion might have?)

The hippo followed Ben's gaze. "Oh, don't worry about the lions," it said. "They won't speak to you. Only a few of us can — only those who were closest to the family. In fact, no one has been able to hear any of us at all since Constance grew up."

"Are you talking about the family in the picture?"

"The very same." The hippo nodded. And it kept on nodding and twinkling as if it expected Ben to say something else. Ben fidgeted on one leg, partly because he was worried about the grown-ups in the office, partly because he felt wary of the hippo. At the same time he was thrilled.

"You're not thinking of going?" said the hippo. "I am so very glad to see you."

"Well . . . I should," Ben replied with another nervous glance at the office door. "My mom'll be expecting me."

Yet he stayed where he was.

"I hope the sengi didn't alarm you," said the hippo. "She's a good creature, but inclined to panic. Stay a little longer. That couple will remain in the office for a while yet — they're having tea and a chat. You know how long *that* can take. And there's so much to tell you. Surely there are some questions you would like to ask?"

"Loads of things. I —"

"Trouble is," said the hippo, "I am famously forgetful. And I didn't know everything even before my great forgetfulness struck me, because I haven't been here that long myself. I only arrived here in 1892. Take a look at my label — it's very fine." It nodded toward the podium where a cream label was attached between its feet.

> ## PYGMY HIPPOPOTAMUS:
> ### CHOEROPSIS LIBERIENSIS. MALE.
>
> *LIBERIA, 1892: Collected by Capt. F. Garner-Gee during his last exploration, which was shortened due to fatal illness. Before his death, the captain specified that the hippo should be placed here where all visitors would see him as they entered the atrium.*

"It's a very nice label," said Ben, "but 1892 is quite a long time ago."

"Is it?" said the hippo. "Well, I certainly can't remember much about it. The bees could help, though; they can recall most things very clearly. They've lived in the crystal hive since this museum opened."

Ben made a face. "I don't much like bees."

"Really? That is most unfortunate. The Garner-Gees were beekeepers long before they became museum keepers."

"They must be very old bees," joked Ben.

"They are the descendants from the first hive," said the hippo. "The great-great-great-great — times two hundred and

70

sixty-eight — grandchildren of those first bees. But they pass all their knowledge down through the generations."

"You mean they have, like, bee historians?"

"In a way." The hippo was nodding again. "They pass their knowledge among themselves using dance steps, which are as precise as your computer codes. They dance to report the news, or to give directions for finding nectar, or to explain how to rear their young, or how to protect the hive. They pass their dances from one bee to the next, so what one knows they all know. They forget little, because the hive has this shared memory that never dies."

"Wow," said Ben. "I thought they just made honey . . . and stung people."

"Indeed, wow," said the hippo with a sigh. "I wish I could dance like them."

Ben wanted to laugh, but he didn't, as the hippo seemed in earnest. Instead he pulled the invitation from his pocket. "The sengi told me the bees delivered this to my house," he said. "D'you know why?"

"I do. Let us say you received it because members of your family are known for their clever ideas."

"Are they?" Ben was astounded.

"They most certainly are," said the hippo. He indicated the office with his head. "Some of us hoped you would be able to help solve our problems. Perhaps you might, as you seem to be able to hear us. And you do have a direct interest in the case...."

"Do I?"

"There is a lot you ought to know...if I could only remember where to start."

"There isn't much time," Ben urged him. "Please try to remember quickly."

"I shall call Flummery," said the hippo. "He's our bee expert, and the only one who can interpret their dances." He began to revolve his ears and then directed a massive snort at the floor so that a cloud of dust was propelled into the hallway. This dust acted like a smoke signal. A short squawk followed in reply, and a moment later the owl from the lobby glided out of the hall. It was flanked by a squadron of bees in a neat V formation. Ben

cringed — scared of the bees — but they swept right past in an elegant loop, spiraling up to the glass roof in a skillful aerobatic maneuver, which ended only when the owl grew confused and crashed. It landed upside down on the hippo's back.

At first it appeared to be stunned. But presently it flipped upright and waved a wing toward the hovering bees. "May I present the Queen's representatives," it hooted. "It is a great honor that they have agreed to dance for you." After that, it glared very hard, so that Ben guessed he was supposed to ignore the crash and say something polite.

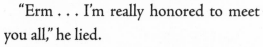

"Erm . . . I'm really honored to meet you all," he lied.

"And allow me," said the hippo. "Ben, let me introduce Flummery, who will interpret the dance for us. We are most honored to have *his* help too. He has made a study of the bee languages and also has a better memory than I."

"Not that anyone could have worse," retorted Flummery. He began to strut pompously along the hippo's back.

"I saw you in the lobby on that clock," Ben blurted out. "And you're in that painting too!"

The owl puffed out his chest feathers. "Well observed — right beside Hector Garner-Gee, because I was his *special* favorite.

That portrait was painted a few years before his father, the captain, died. Very ancient he was by then, but the bees had known him since he was a boy. They say you look like him." He stopped pacing and thrust his face so close that Ben could see each pleated feather around the bird's amber eyes. "There's a lot to tell you. Why don't you sit?"

I can't, thought Ben. *That couple might come out of the office at any moment.*

"Try the steps," murmured the hippo, "and perhaps we could trouble some of the bees to listen at the office door and alert us to any impending departure?"

Immediately a couple of the bees peeled away from the group and headed for the gallery.

"We can rely on them," said the hippo.

And so Ben was persuaded to sit, though he was ill at ease and ready to run.

When he was seated, one of the bees approached. Like a tiny helicopter, it landed square on the dome of the hippo's head. From where Ben sat, the bee looked like a performer on a stage. This was the first time he had watched a bee without flapping his hands or running away. Once he did, he was fascinated.

The bee began intricate movements: a tap with one foot, a twitch from another; a precise pattern played by all six legs, with antennae and wings and a nodding of its head. While it danced, Flummery interpreted these actions into words. Soon Ben hardly noticed the owl at all, as he grew mesmerized. He felt as if he were watching not just one bee but all the other bees that had performed those moves before as well. Indeed, he could almost imagine other future bees dancing those same moves. And although Ben couldn't follow the meaning of the dance, Flummery could, and he told the bees' tale like this....

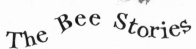

The Bee Stories

CHAPTER 10

Ben Makepeace, this is the story of our museum. Listen well and don't interrupt. You must learn your part in it, for you have one. Our story begins long ago, when our ancestors lived and died in a common wooden hive and the founder of this fine museum was only a boy. In those days they called him Freddie, and he was the kind of child who loved all creatures and rescued many a bee from a sealed window. In return, we often kept him company in his lonely schoolroom. Only we knew that when his tutor left the room,

Freddie pushed his studies aside and opened an ancient book of African legends.

His favorite story was called "The Legend of the Watercow." Freddie read that story again and again, and sometimes he read it aloud, so that many of us carried the tale back to the hive, thinking it might be important. And we were right. It touches all of us. So listen well.

At this point a second bee buzzed forward and joined the first bee on the hippo's head. The first bee retreated to the side, where it vibrated its wings together. This buzzing vibration acted like a drum roll, giving the impression that the owl was about to announce something important. And now Flummery paused, puffed out his feathers, and chanted,

"Now hear ye 'The Legend of the Watercow'!"

In the great green swamps of Western Africa, there lives a solitary creature known as the watercow. By day it wallows in the deeps, thinking so hard that it sleeps. Only as twilight falls does it wake and wander among the thickest trees, feasting on ferns and fruit. It shatters the blackness of the night with the crash of its passing and, more important, with a luminous light. For in its mouth the watercow carries a shining diamond, which guides it on its journey through even the darkest jungle. During the day the watercow buries the jewel in a secret hiding place so that the jewel sleeps too. Only the hunter who can capture the creature at night may take the diamond. And the way will be hard, and the hunting long, but it is a prize well worth the winning: a magical treasure of great virtue, which will bring long life and luck and prosperity to any house it enters, providing it is always safely and secretly kept.

Here the second bee bowed and backed away, and a third bee took up the dance. The owl continued:

Every time Freddie finished reading that story, he spun the globe for luck and vowed, "When I grow up, I'm going to win that diamond and bring that watercow back to my house."

As soon as he was old enough, off he went to Africa, swearing he would do just that, and for a while we heard no more of him. We lived and died in our wooden hive, but we passed our dances on to our young so that eight years later, when Freddie returned, the next generation of bees knew all about him.

To be sure, he had changed: he stood taller, and he went by the name of Captain Garner-Gee, and people treated him with great respect, for he had become a famous explorer and collector. Although he had not found the watercow, his search had led him to discover a host of other creatures, and when he brought them home, there was great excitement among the scientists of that time, for many of those species had never been seen before.

The creatures were dead—that is how specimens were collected in those days—but their skins had been carefully preserved and a taxidermist restored them to their natural shapes, guided by Freddie's detailed drawings. To you that may seem a brutal way to treat rare creatures. Indeed, it is atrocious. But in those days only the very rich could travel far and wide. And there were no devices to view creatures from other parts of the world, so taxidermy was thought to be the ideal means of classifying the beasts of the earth. We have heard that you can find exhibits like these in museums across the world, which are used even now for scientific research. All the same, in those early days, Captain Freddie kept his collection to himself in his own home.

With his next shipment there came a wife, though she was alive, to be sure. Her name was Patience, and she was patient by nature as well as by name, which was lucky for us, because she became our beekeeper.

It was lucky for the captain too, because, in time, the house filled with Garner-Gee children, and when those children grew, they all began collecting too. In a few decades, the house was full to bursting.

Patience bore the chaos without complaint until the summer of 1866, when a giraffe arrived. It wasn't the only giraffe — in fact, it was the eighth — and it was very large. Unfortunately, on the way indoors, it became wedged — stuck half in and half out of the parlor window — just when Great-Aunt Myrtle arrived for tea. Aunt Myrtle was a sensitive fool. She fainted clean away. They had to use a saw to remove the giraffe, so the tea party was not a success, and this time

Patience lost her temper. She never had before, not in all those years, but that day she shouted, "This is the last straw!" She seemed as angry as a black hornet as she fumed, "Not one more article is coming into this house! Not until some of it leaves."

And the family could see that she meant it. Even the captain, who could be fierce enough when he chose, merely remarked, "You're right, my dear. It's time we shared our collection with the public. I've always planned to build my own museum."

And that was the beginning of the Gee Museum — his greatest project.

As the fourth bee took up the story, the others hovered in a line, thrumming their wings so that Ben was conscious of a humming on several notes. It was rather like a fanfare from tiny breathy bagpipes, and it made this section of the story seem the most significant.

It didn't happen overnight. Creating the Gee Museum took an age. The captain couldn't do it alone. There were years of construction and cabinet making, years spent classifying and labeling, while the captain — like a great spider in a monumental web — tempted his three sons to help him. First came Hector as his chief assistant, then Humphrey joined them as a curator. Eventually Montgomery and Patience became entangled too. After all, the family had lived with the collection their whole lives, so they knew better than most how to hang a whale skeleton, or classify a grasshopper, or arrange small mammals in sound scientific order.

Even we bees were recruited. For in the heart of the insect room, the captain built our crystal hive. It was a peace offering to Patience, because she loved us, and once she moved our queen inside, naturally our colony followed.

The first year was a difficult time for us bees, as we had no dances to instruct us about our new neighborhood, so honey was sparse that winter. But we survived. And the following summer the hive prospered. Then we built a wax city that was finer than anything the captain could ever construct.

And while we built, the insect room grew around the crystal hive, and the museum grew around the insect room. Then the collections began to arrive by the cartload. Eventually, in 1877, the crates had all gone. The Gee Museum was ready to be opened to the public.

The bees changed shift again: the others backed away and were silent as a fifth bee landed on the hippo's head. Ben noticed this one moved more slowly; its yellow stripes were faded, and its wings were frayed at the edges. It began its dance with a question.

Why do humans collect things? Once they own them, they only seek more. Do they think that by parading their possessions, they can slow the slip and slide of time? If so, they are fools, for all things perish and disperse. We bees have no need of collections. As we age and our wings disintegrate, we are satisfied to have contributed to our tribe — which will survive us.

Yet as Captain Garner-Gee grew older, he did not grow wiser, like a bee. Instead of thinking of his children and his grandchildren and his grandchildren's children, he could only mumble about what he had not done in his own life. He spoke of the watercow again, convincing himself that the museum only had a future if the watercow stood in the central court. We were saddened, but not surprised, when he headed back to Africa in search of it.

He was gone three winters. He sent no news. The family feared he had perished. When he did return, he was gravely ill, bitten by a tsetse fly and suffering from a sleeping sickness. He survived long enough to supervise the very few specimens he brought back from that last expedition, but as far as we know, there was no beast that went by the name of a watercow.

All the same, just before he died, the captain insisted that he had captured the creature and acquired the diamond for the museum. But by then he was delirious. Nevertheless, after his death, the three brothers searched high and searched low, but no diamond was ever found. In the end no one believed it existed — except for Patience, who always maintained it was secretly hidden somewhere so that its power would safeguard the prosperity and long life of the Gee Museum.

At that moment, they were all startled by a hollow voice that issued from the gramophone horn. It was a snide and rather lazy voice. It said, "I hate to mention the obvious, but if the diamond is here safeguarding the museum, why are we in so much trouble?"

The Chameleon

CHAPTER 11

"Hello, Leon," said the hippo. "I wondered when you would show yourself."

A patch of gray inside the speaker horn flushed green and stretched until it became apparent that it was a chameleon.

He slunk onto the podium, fixing one bulging eye on Ben. The other black-dot pupil swiveled independently as it tracked the bees.

"I have listened very patiently," the chameleon said with some contempt, "and it seems we have the right boy, since he can hear us well enough. But why are you wasting time? He doesn't need a history lesson. Tell him what he ought to do and let's get on with it."

"You can't rush bees," squawked Flummery.

"Can't you?"

Leon's tongue shot out like a rocket and recoiled with a bee captured on one end. The bee had no chance, for a chameleon has an incredible tongue, twice the length of its body, with a bulbous ball of muscle at the end like a suction cup, which can move at ballistic speed — faster than a fighter jet.

Naturally the other bees arose in a fury.

"Where's your respect?" Flummery hooted.

Leon turned his back. Languidly he plucked the bee from his tongue and dangled the struggling insect above his bucket-like mouth, murmuring, "Shall I swallow you? Shall I bite you in half and nibble your wings? I might if your fuzzy-buzzy pals don't end their silly story."

"Let it go," demanded the hippo. "Ben has a right to hear this."

"Ben has a right to leave before those *ghastly* people find him here," said Leon. "That man is a greedy bully, which is bad, but the woman has the eyes of a fanatic. I fear she is an addict."

"What d'you mean?" asked Ben.

The hippo was looking concerned. "Leon may be right," he said with a sigh. "She has that look. Collecting is generally a harmless human habit. Occasionally, though, the collector is consumed by a vile compulsion, a dark desire that eats into their soul until they will stop at nothing in order to possess more. When that happens, they can never be satisfied."

Ben gulped. "Is Miss Snow that kind of person?"

"Perhaps," said the hippo. "She has an obsessive glint in her eyes that we have seen before. It's the sign of a desperate desire for something, and if she thinks you are in her way, maybe it would be wiser if she didn't see you."

"So let's get on with it," said Leon. "Show the boy the silver bottle, have him open it up, then let him go before they catch him."

Ben stood up, ready to leave. "*What* silver bottle?"

"Don't go near that bottle," twittered the owl.

"I haven't even *seen* a bottle."

"This bee seems quite upset!" remarked Leon, swinging the bee by one wing.

The owl dived at him. "You're a disgrace," he screeched.

But the chameleon simply dodged, scuttling to the floor.

"Oh, let the bee go," said the hippo. "We must finish the story. There may be some urgency."

"Some urgency?" the chameleon mimicked. Yet he freed the bee, which indignantly fled, and then, with an angry buzzing, the whole group flew off to join the bees in the gallery.

Flummery blinked slowly enough for Ben to see the tiny layered feathers on his eyelids. "Well, that was foolish," he said. "We may need their help."

The chameleon sighed theatrically. "Oh, *puh-leaze*. Do get on with it, if you *really* think the boy needs to hear this tedious family saga."

"Maybe you could speed it up a bit," said Ben anxiously.

Flummery shifted his wings and scowled, but he took up the story again.

"The bees were explaining what happened after the captain died. It was all right at first, you know — the fortunes of the museum ran smoothly for a while. But then came the arguments. Hector wanted the museum to continue purely as a natural-history collection, but his brothers wanted to diversify — they'd had enough of hunting. Humphrey began by bringing in a collection of valuable clocks and the scientific instruments. Hector didn't mind those so much. But then Montgomery added all manner of unsavory curiosities. For a start, he expanded that ridiculous bottle collection."

"Hush," said the hippo, opening one eye. "Flummery, do not take sides, or you will be behaving as badly as the brothers did. Ben, I do remember this: Hector had no respect for Montgomery's ideas, and one night the two of them had a terrible fight. The museum was damaged and Montgomery left forever. He went about as far as he could go."

"Where did he go?" asked Ben.

The owl explained, "There's a set of remote islands in the Pacific Ocean, which I believe are now known as Micronesia, though they used to have another name. That is where he went."

"Very far away," said the hippo, nodding. "The family lost contact with him."

"And I wish he'd taken that spooky silver bottle with him," said Flummery. "It gives me the quiveryflibbets every time I'm near it."

"But he didn't take it," said the hippo. "It's still here in the bottle room. He took none of the collection, as far as we know. Yet when he left, he somehow took the heart of the place with him — or at least I always felt it was so. As did Patience."

"She never got over the loss of her youngest son," agreed

Flummery. "She died soon afterward, leaving the museum in the hands of Hector and Humphrey, and her granddaughter, of course, Hector's only child —"

"The girl in the picture?" Ben asked.

"The girl in the picture." The hippo nodded. "She ensured that Montgomery's curious collections stayed in the museum, and once she grew up, she became the greatest curator the museum ever had. But neither she nor Humphrey ever married, so there were no more Garner-Gee children to inherit the museum."

"But what happened to Montgomery?"

"You're a sharp boy," said Flummery. "But remember, there was a war. It turned the world upside down and nothing was heard of Montgomery for a generation. Nevertheless, Constance discovered that he had married and had a family overseas. There was a grandson — an explorer and sea captain. And like all the Gees, he was full of clever ideas. One day, not so long ago, he sailed right back here."

The owl paused then and gazed at Ben. The others were silent too, but all three watched him intently.

Ben felt very uncomfortable. "If the museum will belong to Montgomery's grandson, why isn't he here saving it now?" he blurted out.

"He can't," said Flummery softly.

"He's dead," said Leon.

The hippo's eyes were full of compassion. "Constance met him only once — just before he died."

"He was drowned," said Leon, and both his golden-sequin eyes focused hard on Ben. "Lost at sea."

"Like Dad," mumbled Ben.

"Exactly," said Leon, watching Ben with interest. "Exactly."

A Witch in a Bottle

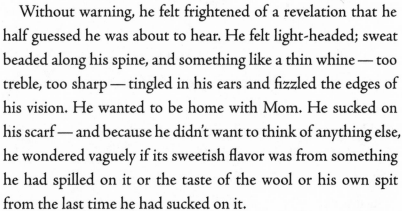

CHAPTER 12

Drowned, thought Ben. *Like my dad.*

Without warning, he felt frightened of a revelation that he half guessed he was about to hear. He felt light-headed; sweat beaded along his spine, and something like a thin whine — too treble, too sharp — tingled in his ears and fizzled the edges of his vision. He wanted to be home with Mom. He sucked on his scarf — and because he didn't want to think of anything else, he wondered vaguely if its sweetish flavor was from something he had spilled on it or the taste of the wool or his own spit from the last time he had sucked on it.

"Too much for the boy," the hippo murmured. "I told you he was too young to take on all this. We should have waited."

"I'm not too young," said Ben, though his voice cracked.

"We couldn't wait," said the owl. "We had to act immediately."

As if to confirm the urgency, the bees were suddenly among them again, and it seemed to Ben there was an anxious whine in their buzzing. Glancing upstairs, he saw that the office door remained closed, but the sengi was leaping down the steps so

quickly that her motion seemed double-speed. Long before she reached them, she began to squeak: "Constance has agreed to read their wicked papers. She's lost faith in the museum — I could see it in her eyes — she's never bothered to look at any papers before. She's been tricked! Or maybe she *wants* to be tricked. There's no hope for us now. The boy came too late."

"Calm yourself," said the hippo to the shrew as she scampered in an agitated circle. "There's no such thing as too late. There's always time in the future."

"Oh, do zip it," snapped the chameleon. "Time for some action maybe. Get the boy to open the silver bottle before he goes home. I'll do the rest."

The lines on the hippo's face deepened. "That would be a very bad idea."

"The diamond . . ." began Flummery.

But now the sengi quivered with impatience. "Diamond!" she exclaimed breathlessly. "It's too late for that and you know it. We've searched every nook and cranny, but there's never been any sign of it, never-never-never-never-never-*never*!"

The chameleon examined his long fingers. "I do agree, dear lady, but try telling these clods . . ."

Ben was still feeling queasy. "I have to go," he said as the animals squabbled. "*They'll* be coming out soon."

"Of course you should go," said the chameleon, sidling toward him. "But how about a little favor first? All you have to do is open a teeny-tiny bottle."

"Don't!" screeched the owl.

"Rash," agreed the hippo. "Ben, don't touch it."

Leon looked sulky. "It won't take a minute. Do be a sport; I'd do it myself — I can undo locks — but I can't quite get my fingers . . ."

"What's in the bottle?" Ben asked.

The sengi bared her needlelike teeth at all of them. "Haven't you even told him *that* yet?"

"Hold your horseflies — we don't know if there *is* a witch in the bottle," squawked the owl.

"A witch!" Ben exclaimed.

"Rumored to be."

"According to the label."

"We don't know for sure, because it came to the museum already sealed. It may be empty."

"And it may not be," squeaked the sengi. "My fur stands on end whenever I go near it."

"Well . . . exactly," said Flummery. "And what if opening the bottle makes matters worse? What then, eh? And it very well *could* make things worse — if there's a witch inside it. I mean, it depends on the mood of this possible witch, doesn't it? Bless my feathers, a witch like that would probably be accustomed to casting wild magic. That's chaotic. No telling what might happen if you let *that* loose in here."

"Yet if there is a witch inside the bottle, she's a part of this museum," fretted the sengi. "She might help us save it."

"She might be very grateful if we released her," the chameleon said slyly. "Wishes have followed in similar cases. Genies, for instance, are said to be generous."

98

"That was a genie in a lamp," said the sengi. "Might not be the same with witches in bottles. What if she comes out in a festering temper?"

"My point exactly," said Flummery, and the bees buzzed in an agitated clot around his head as if they agreed.

Leon swiveled one eye at the sengi. "Whose side are you on?"

"The side of sense," the hippo cut in curtly. "There are some objects that are best left alone, and that bottle is one of them. Let's take no more risks. We've found the boy. Once Constance meets him, everything will change. With Ben by her side, she'll feel strong enough to send those people away, and —"

"No!" cried Ben. "I'm not going to be by her side. My mom will want me home. In fact —"

He stopped. He had spoken too loudly. Now they heard a chair scraping the floor in the office, and the hasty tap of high-heeled shoes. Only the hippo remained on his plinth. The other animals scattered before the office door flew open.

Tara Snow flew to the balustrade. "There!" she shrieked, leaning over the edge. "It's that boy."

"Now, don't you worry, Miss Garner-Gee," growled Julian Pike, coming up behind her — he was moving alarmingly fast for such a large man. "I'll escort this trespasser off the premises."

"Better run!" the hippo whispered.

It was certainly too late to hide, so Ben fled.

He dived for the hall, passing the mystery doorways, feet drumming on the wooden floor, past the cabinet of eggs, past the painting. He skidded to a halt at the front door, bewildered at the many knobs and bolts.

While he hesitated, he heard a scrabbling sound nearby and then the door swung open of its own accord. Ben decided it must have been ajar and had caught in the wind. Anyway, there was only time to think about running, so he leaped across the threshold and galloped down the steps to his bike.

The doors slammed behind him. He breathed in lungfuls of fresh air and reality. He smelled wet leaves and fog. He heard the roar of distant traffic and ordinary life — it was such a relief.

From indoors he heard the doorknob rattle. But by then he was astride his bike and speeding into the twilight.

And it was past dinnertime.

He pedaled like the wind for home.

Eggs for Dinner

CHAPTER 13

"Where've you been?" said Mom. Her voice was like ice.

Ben had rehearsed what he'd say. "I'm sorry I'm late, but —" He stopped. "Mom?" She looked greenish-white and anxious. He rushed to hug her. "I'm sorry," he said again. "I went to that museum. You didn't say I couldn't — but then I couldn't get in, and then I did, but —"

"Do you realize how worried I've been?" Her voice cracked. "And today of all days."

Ben saw that papers from the shop were still strewn over the table. Usually the table would be set by now. Something was wrong.

"What do you mean, today of all days?"

Mom's lips were pressed together into a tight line, as though she were trying not to cry. She was clutching a letter. Now she dropped it onto the table. There was something despairing about her gesture. Ben reached for the letter. She snatched it back. Then the scolding stopped and she hugged him.

"At least you're home safe," she said. "So long as you're safe, nothing can be too bad."

Ben found this more worrying than when she'd been angry. "I'm not that late," he said. "What's happened? Why is today different?"

Her shoulders slumped.

"Tell me!"

She sighed. "I only got around to opening the mail this afternoon. There's another letter from the landlord. It's what I was worried about: he's sold our building to a property developer called Pike Developments."

"Pike!"

"Yes, it's a nasty name, isn't it? And they've got a dreadful reputation. They make it very difficult for tenants to stay when they want to develop an area. They'll do what they can to get rid of us."

"Pike Developments?" said Ben. "Is that *Julian* Pike?"

"Yes . . . I think that's his name. How on earth d'you know that?" Mom drew out a pan and put it on the stove. Ben guessed they'd be having eggs again—

they always had eggs when Mom hadn't sold much in the shop.

"That man, that Julian Pike . . . I saw him today," he said.

"Don't be silly."

"*I did.* He was at the museum. He wants to knock that down too and —"

"He . . . what! How do you know? What have you been doing?" Mom looked aghast. "I knew I shouldn't have let you go near that place. How did you meet him?"

"I didn't exactly meet him."

"Then who *exactly* did you meet? What did you hear?"

"Lots," said Ben carefully. "I heard some bad things about that man, and some things that . . ." He paused, and then in a rush he cried, "I think they were about my dad. He took me there when I was little, didn't he? I remember it."

She looked away, chewing the side of her fist.

"Please, Mom."

"I think he took you once," she muttered. She opened the fridge and took out the eggs. As she put three into the pan, she added, "So, was the old lady there? I can't believe it. I don't understand how she can still be alive."

"She is. I saw her. But . . . I didn't speak to her either."

"Then who did you speak to?"

Now it was Ben who avoided answering. He knew Mom wouldn't believe the truth. He watched her cutting bread, attacking the loaf as if the slices might rise up like bread soldiers and fight. It didn't seem the best time to mention talking animals. Instead he said daringly, "I need to know about my dad." Then he scuttled off to fetch the silverware and glasses.

The blue flames from the stove top hissed against the pan as Mom rummaged in the cupboard for eggcups. He watched her spooning the eggs out: one for her, two for him. She motioned him to sit and sat down heavily herself. "Ben, I'm exhausted, and I've got a headache. I know there are things you want to know. It's time I told you more — and I promised myself I would, soon. You're old enough now, but it's so complicated, and it's been quite a day — I'm too tired tonight."

Ben stared at his eggs. Then he picked up his spoon and bashed the tops of them really hard.

Mom sliced her own open and reached over to rescue his. Then she turned on the TV.

Ben was starving. He had a vague feeling he ought to be too upset to eat, but he dunked a piece of bread into that liquid-dandelion yolk. The bread was crusty and fresh. The butter mingled with the egg and salt, and though there was a bit of a crunch from the mauled eggshells that had ended up inside the egg, it still tasted delicious. He gobbled it up, rammed his spoon through the bottom of the first shell to break it, then began on his second.

Mom looked calmer once she had eaten. As usual, when she finished, she left her spoon in her shell, tempting him to reach over and push it through the bottom. This was a game they often played, so he knew that she'd whisk it away before he could break it. But Ben wasn't playing silly games tonight.

Instead he said abruptly, "You never tell me anything about Dad. I don't even know where he grew up."

To his utter surprise she gave him an answer: "Not here," she said. "His grandfather was English, but your dad grew up on the other side of the world."

Ben hardly dared breathe in case she stopped talking.

"If you must know," she added, "he grew up on an island called Yap — yes, it's an odd name. It's in Micronesia — oh, you may well gasp. I'd be surprised if you've heard of it. I hadn't."

"Someone . . . mentioned Micronesia," mumbled Ben.

"It's a group of islands in the Pacific," said Mom. "That's the big blue ocean that covers so much of the globe. His father was some sort of scientist there; so was his grandfather, come to think of it."

"There's no chance he's still alive?" Ben blurted out.

"No chance."

That sounded very final, but Ben wasn't going to let her stop now. "How do you know?"

"Well, no one knows absolutely for certain, but they found something in some wreckage — that stone, the one with the hole bored in it."

"The one you gave me on my birthday?"

"Yes." She turned to him again. "I did intend to tell you more about it."

"Tell me now. Please!" Ben urged.

The Shipwrecked Stone

CHAPTER 14

"Someone found a sealed plastic box adrift among the wreckage of a boat," said Mom. "It had my name and address on it, and the stone was in there too. I knew then that your dad must have known he wasn't going to survive or he would never have taken it off. He was so superstitious about that stone — I mean, when he went sailing, he always wore it for luck. He used to hang it around his neck on a shoelace, said it had been his father's before him and his grandfather's before that. He used to say he wanted you to have it on your tenth birthday."

"But when you gave it to me, you never told me what it was!" said Ben.

"I'm telling you now." She looked directly at him then and sighed. "Ben, I'm sorry. I know I should've told you more. But . . . sometimes grown-ups feel so sad that it almost makes them ill.

107

Losing someone you love . . . it's like . . . it can feel like losing a limb. And did you know that people who have lost a leg or an arm often feel pain in that leg, even though it isn't there anymore? It's a bit like that for me. It still hurts to talk about your dad."

"But I lost him too."

"I know you did, love. I know that." She rubbed her forehead. He saw that her other hand was clenched tight. "But when it happened, you were so little. I couldn't be ill because I still had you. I had to make a good home for you, and I had to do it every single day, no matter how sad I felt. If I thought about your dad too much, I . . . Look, I know it sounds like I'm making excuses, but I tried not to think too much and that's how I got by. I know it's time I told you more about your dad, and I will, but not tonight, Ben. I'm exhausted and I still have a lot of work to do."

She hugged him. Then she stood up and began clearing the plates. A story came on the TV news about a river bursting its banks, and she turned to give it her whole attention.

But Ben wasn't going to allow this conversation to end. "Just one more thing . . . *please* . . ."

She sighed.

"Why do I have your last name?"

"Because you're my son."

"But what was his name? Was it Garner-Gee?"

"That's two things."

"Did you ever meet Miss Garner-Gee?"

"Ben, *please*! That's enough! I told you. I've still got so much to do."

No, it's not enough, thought Ben in silent fury. *Not nearly enough.*

The news droned on: more floods somewhere in the north, then a story about the terrible damage that floodwater could inflict on buildings if they weren't cleared quickly. Ben glanced at Mom and saw that she looked tearful.

"I thought you might have fallen into the weir," she whispered.

"I'm not that stupid," he retorted. He felt tears spring to his own eyes and angrily blinked them away. But truth be told, he'd had enough for one day too — and then Mom was spooning out apple crumble, and a TV program about equatorial rain forests was about to begin.

"Can we talk about Dad tomorrow night, then? When I get home from school?"

"Ben, I'm sorry, but I won't be in when you come back from school. I've got to close the shop early. There's a meeting with that property developer. Half the street is attending. It's not only our shop that's in trouble — Pike owns the whole block now."

"Can you stop him?" Ben asked.

"I don't know." Mom shrugged. "We're not sure exactly what we're stopping yet either. He may not want to build immediately. But I should look through the lease before tomorrow, so . . ."

"OK," said Ben. The apple crumble had ice cream with it, and the TV program had begun. "After you get back from the meeting then?"

Before bed that night, Ben went to his shelf of special objects and reexamined the blue stone with the hole that Mom had given him on his birthday. The stone was semitransparent, like a half-sucked piece of hard candy, and its shape was organic. It looked more like something that had been washed up on a beach than something crafted.

He held it to his eye.

Now his room floated in underwater blue, distant and magical. He examined the rest of his collection shelf. His treasures — mostly common rocks and a few beachcombed fossils — looked rare and precious now.

"Ben, are you in bed yet?" called Mom.

"Nearly."

He put the stone back and rummaged in the bottom of his closet for a shoelace. He found one of the dress shoes that Mom liked and he didn't. It had a leather lace, so he unlooped it, then threaded it through the stone. He looked at it, trying to remember if Dad had been wearing it around his neck the day they had gone to the museum together. Tying it around his own neck, he looked at his reflection in his bedroom window.

The orange streetlight outside was transforming raindrops on the window into little yellowish drops of light. *A yellow light means get ready to go*, he thought.

For what?

Would they have to move?

He screwed up his face, trying not to cry. The shop and apartment were all he remembered, and Mom had worked so hard to make the shop a success.

Was it a success?

"Yes!" he muttered. "We'd be fine if the rent hadn't gone up so much." And he squashed down all thoughts of the unpaid bills, and only enough money for eggs for dinner, and Mom's worried face, and he thought of Julian Pike and his bulldozers with loathing. But how could a boy and his mom get the better of a man like that?

Then he thought of Tara Snow and her goggling, hypnotic stare. He'd have to get the better of her too. He held the blue stone up to his eye again. Now the window dripped green instead of yellow.

Green for go? he thought.

There *was* something he could do. He could try using magic. He could open that silver bottle. Yesterday morning he would have laughed away any talk of witches and magic, but tonight he wasn't so confident. In fact, he felt a bit scared. He unlooped the lace from around his neck and put the stone back on the shelf.

How do you know if a witch is good or bad? he wondered.

Mom knocked quietly on his door. Ben tried to rub away any signs of tears from his face as she came in. She sat on his bed and hugged him, and looked so fragile and headachy that he couldn't bear to press her for any more information. Besides, he wanted to comfort her; truth be told, he wanted some comfort himself. So in an effort to make her stay longer, he mentioned a story with a witch in it that used to be his favorite when he was younger.

"Tell me your egg story," he said.

She smiled then, and he guessed she was relieved it was all he had asked.

"I thought you said you were too old for that nowadays."

"I am."

She laughed. "It's OK to still want bedtime stories now and then," she said. "They're a comfort for grown-ups too, you know. That one reminds me of our happiest times, when we locked the world away and were just us."

"Tell it again," said Ben.

And this is the tale his mom told in her lovely, sad singsong voice.

Mom's Egg Story

There was once a girl who noticed that when people ate eggs, they usually broke up the shells.

"Why do they do that?" asked the girl. She was eating boiled eggs with her granny at the time.

The granny replied, "People often do things without thinking or without remembering the real reason they do them."

"What is the real reason?" said the girl. "Do you know?"

"There's a rhyme about it," said her granny, and she sang this song:

Make a hole in the shell, my dear,
Or a witch will make a boat, I fear,
Then over the water far from home,
Through the night the witch will roam.

Well, the girl thought about that, and then replied, "I don't see why the poor witches shouldn't have boats if they want. We have boats." And quick as a wink, she ran to the open window, lobbed her eggshell through it, and cried, "Witch, here is your boat."

To her amazement, she saw the shell whipped up by the wind and whisked so high that it disappeared into the clouds, while a thin, high voice called out, "I thank you."

The granny was upset. "No good will come of this," she warned, and for a few nights the girl was frightened, but after that she forgot all about it.

Many years later, when she had grown to be a young woman, she rowed out to an island to gather herbs. While she was busy, a sudden tempest hit the beach and a great wave washed her boat away. The tide rose higher and higher until only a tiny tip of the island was above the flood, and the poor young woman thought she would drown.

She had almost given up hope when she saw an odd white boat riding the waves, bobbing and paddling toward her. The skipper was a woman with wild violet eyes and the coxswain who steered was a black cat — or at least the young woman thought it was a cat, though it seemed to have extra limbs.

"Jump in!" they said.

And the young woman did, as what choice did she have? Without another word, they swept through the storm, scudding over the waves with more seacraft than ever a master seaman could muster. Only when they reached the shore did the witch speak.

"When your feet tread the dry earth, you must turn three times widdershins and at each turn look at my boat," she said.

Well, the young woman was so grateful, she did just that; at each turn she looked at the boat, and at each glance the boat grew smaller, until it was the size of an egg. Then the now-tiny witch shook the rusty corkscrews of her hair and sang in a high, thin voice:

> *This is the shell you threw to me.*
> *Even a witch can grateful be.*

And so singing, she vanished: cat, shell, and all, leaving the young woman alone and safe on the beach.

After telling the story, Mom kissed Ben good night. There was something he wished he could say to her as she went. He had said it once, but he never would again because it had made her sad. He wanted to say, *I wish a witch had rescued my dad.*

But that night he just said, "It isn't true, is it?"

"Of course it isn't true."

"But you never put a hole in your eggshells."

"It's just a bit of fun," Mom said with a laugh. "An old superstition — I've told you that. I used to believe it when I was young, but then I stopped believing — like you did."

"But the witch was a good one — wasn't she?"

"That's what I always thought," said Mom softly. Then she hugged him one last time, and whispering "Good night," she left with a smile in her voice.

However, Ben felt as guilty as a fox.

This was because he had decided that he was going to go

back to the museum the next day. He had to. He was gambling that it would be one of those third Mondays in the month when the museum was open. Even then, it would only be open until four o'clock.

"But it's now or never," he told himself, thinking of the words on the back of the ticket.

Nevertheless, going there tomorrow meant he would have to miss school to arrive before it closed. He would be skipping school for the first time ever.

He sat up. Surely they'd phone Mom if he didn't turn up.

Unless he left after lunch.

They wouldn't be able to phone Mom in the afternoon, because she'd be out at that meeting. And Mom didn't have a cell phone since her last one had broken, and she hadn't had the money to replace it.

He waited until he heard her go to bed.

He waited until he thought she'd be asleep.

Then, feeling treacherous, he slunk out of bed, tiptoed past her room, and sneaked upstairs to the shop.

He had taken the blue stone along with him for luck, and as he sat down, he tucked it carefully to one side of the computer. In the glow of the screen, he tapped away with nervous sweaty hands. After a moment he found the template Mom used for shop letters and began to type:

Dear Mrs. Conway,

Ben has to go to the dentist.

He must leave school at 2 o'clock.

I will meet him there.

Yours sincerely,

Sara Makepeace

The printer uttered a mechanical groan as the letter slid out. Ben froze. No sound from Mom. Ben looked at the letter. He decided it was quite good. He crept back to his room and hid it in his school bag. After that he slept like a hippo. If he had not been so sleepy, perhaps he would have realized that he hadn't deleted the letter on the computer.

A Bottle of Trouble

CHAPTER 16

When Ben arrived at the museum that Monday afternoon, he hid his bike in a rhododendron bush near the hive entrance.

"Look after my bike," he whispered up to the hive when a couple of bees appeared. Then he fled for the front door. He still wasn't comfortable around bees, but he was uncomfortable everywhere that day because he felt horribly guilty about missing school.

What if Mom finds out? he worried. *And what about Mrs. Conway?* Ben felt especially guilty about his teacher — she had been so trusting when he handed her the forged note. At school everyone thought he was a good kid.

Was he a good kid?

Today he'd been so sneaky, so dishonest, yet he still didn't know if the museum would be open. While he was dithering on the steps, the great doors swung apart. He took that as his answer and nipped through them before anyone spotted him.

This time the ticket booth glowed with an amber light. Amber reflections gilded the clocks, gleamed on the glass, glittered in the eyes of the birds so that they seemed knowing — as if they knew Ben should have been at school.

"Hello?" he croaked to whoever might be listening.

Nobody answered.

But presently he noticed there was a call bell on the counter that hadn't been there the day before. It had a sign next to it. Taking care to avoid the brass trip button on the second flagstone, Ben crept over to read the sign:

We are open
Today
Please ring
for attention.

Did he want attention, though?

He looked around for Flummery and was dismayed to see that the owl's perch on top of the casement clock was empty. What a blow. He had been planning to discuss the blue stone with the owl; indeed, he had been thinking about it all morning. Biting the skin on the side of his thumb, he wondered what to do instead. He decided he ought to find Miss Garner-Gee. But before that, since he seemed to be quite alone, he would take a quick peek at the bottle room. He only intended to check it out. He couldn't see the harm in that.

As Ben walked down the hallway, he could hear other visitors in the atrium. Soon he saw a small girl in a pink rain jacket crossing behind the hippo. Her mother followed. With any luck, they would distract the hippo while Ben sidled into the bottle room.

The room was small and dark, with a low ceiling and no windows. The air in there smelled musty, and slightly sweet, and wrong. Ben thought it looked like a witch's store cupboard, for shelved on the walls from ceiling to floor were a multitude of lugubrious specimens: bottled toads, and pickled lizards, and frogs, and slugs, and many types of

spotted newts, and seahorses, and numerous snakes, and several species of octopuses. Every bottle had been labeled in the same neat handwritten print. Each contained something different, yet their contents looked remarkably similar, as most of the creatures had faded to the pallor of uncooked chicken and glowed softly in their amber brew like a drowned demon army.

But all of these were glass specimen jars and bottles. Ben couldn't see a single silver bottle.

Actually, he felt relieved, because he wanted to leave this room. There was something unpleasant about it: the shadows seemed thick with questions and secrets, and he felt as if all those bottled fungoid creatures were watching to see what he would do next.

Just as he was about to go, a reflection flickered yellow across all the glass surfaces. Something had moved behind him.

He spun to face a table cabinet. He hadn't noticed it earlier because it was positioned behind the door. Leon was climbing onto its glass tabletop. He must have

intended to be visible, for his skin was decked out in the colors of a ripe banana.

"Hello, Leon," Ben said warily.

The chameleon turned his head to watch Ben from over his shoulder. One golden eye was focused on Ben, but he directed the other to the cabinet as he climbed on top of it.

"Care to take a peek?"

"Why?" said Ben, though he'd guessed why. He began to say, "The hippo and Flummery said I shouldn't —"

"But since you're here . . ." Leon coaxed, both black-dot pupils fixed on Ben. "After all, nobody said you shouldn't *look*. Isn't that why you came in here?"

Ben couldn't resist. He shuffled closer. He saw that this cabinet was full of bottles too, but these didn't belong with the specimen bottles. These were curiosities, displayed together only because they were all bottles of one sort or another. One of them contained a fully rigged ship; another, which was misted in algae, held a message inked onto an old piece of parchment. There was a cluster of Bohemian glass perfume bottles in tints of cranberry, amber, and lavender; there were blue apothecaries' bottles labeled *Poison*, and there was a bottle made of pink quartz filled with distilled roses. Farther along the row, a pale-green bottle bore a label marked *Bottle for collecting tears*; another displayed a slug impaled on a thorn, and next to that was a brown bottle, which apparently held a charm for clearing warts.

The chameleon shifted to reveal that he was sitting directly over a bulbous silver bottle. When Ben bent to read the angular writing on that label, the hairs on the back of his neck rose.

Silvered and stoppered bottle said to contain a witch. Obtained by Montgomery Garner-Gee from an old lady living in a village near Hove, Sussex, who remarked "and they do say there be a witch in it, and if you let 'un out there'll be a peck o' trouble."

"I don't need any more trouble," Ben said, stepping backward.

"Not tempted, then? Even when it's almost under your paws?"

"I bet nothing would happen if I did open it."

"And what will happen if you don't open it?"

"Why hasn't Miss Garner-Gee?"

"Who knows? Sometimes she pretends not to believe in magic; other times she says the bottle would be spoiled if it were uncapped. The truth is, she's never had the nerve. You're our last hope . . . and your mother's. Poor us."

127

"There's the diamond," Ben blustered. "What if we found that instead?"

"Pixieshine," said the chameleon.

"And a witch in a bottle isn't?" said Ben nervously.

"What a timid turtle you are," said Leon. "Your father had more courage. He'd have opened it like a shot if he'd ever come back."

"What do you know about my dad?"

"Haven't you figured that out yet? Dear me, the others were so sure you'd have worked it out for yourself, but — as you're clearly not the brightest of bunnies — I suppose it's my duty to tell you —"

But in fact he didn't tell Ben anything. This was because a child came running down the hallway. The chameleon skittered down the table leg and squirmed through the metal grate in the floor.

"What were you going to say?" asked Ben urgently. He knelt down to the grate.

"Ask me later. Constance is coming," hissed the chameleon.

Outside in the hallway, the child scampered past the door.

Two pairs of grown-up feet followed more sedately. Ben could hear the adults' voices echoing in the larger space of the egg room. They were saying goodbye in that grown-up rambling way that can go on and on. The child stomped in boredom.

"They've gone right past. Please come out," Ben begged.

But Leon had disappeared.

Ben stood up. The grown-ups talked. The girl stomped again. He felt drawn to the bottle; it was a strange feeling, as if both he and it were faintly magnetic. He knew that the cabinet would be locked, so he wasn't seriously trying to open it when he tugged experimentally around the lid.

It wasn't locked. It sprang up.

It was a large lid and, being also a tabletop, was awkward to hold and very heavy. Ben tried to close it but the catch seemed stuck, so he had to continue to prop it up, and he panicked because he knew if he were to drop it hard, the glass might break. In the end he pushed it all the way up until it rested against the wall. Then he tried to fix the catch.

Without the barrier of the glass, the bottle looked more substantial: the brindled silver gleamed, the milky stopper glowed. He couldn't resist reaching out to touch the curved edge of it. And the instant he did, he longed to hold it.

Before he picked it up, he promised himself he would put it back immediately. It felt smooth and unexpectedly warm as he cradled it in his palms. It looked very old. The silver had a yellowed moonlike glow to it. The stopper looked solidly sealed. That was good; he didn't think he could have opened the bottle if he'd wanted. That being so, he couldn't help giving it an experimental wiggle . . .

Pop!

The stopper came out between Ben's fingers!

Constance Garner-Gee

CHAPTER 17

He half expected green smoke or sparks. There were none. Nothing happened at all.

"There's no witch," Ben told himself in a whisper. Yet he noticed a slight metallic, thunderstorm scent. And he couldn't rid himself of the impression that something had changed—like the silence in a room when someone has just left it.

The front door slammed as the last visitors of the day left the museum. The old lady was returning. Ben's fingers fumbled as he tried to jam the stopper back into the bottle; the stopper was oddly resistant, so that by the time he had resealed it her footsteps were very close. Yet here was the cabinet still wide open!

He bumped the lid down, flinching at the sound. Luckily this time the catch worked smoothly, but somehow—and he never could decide afterward how he could have been so stupid—he had forgotten to put the bottle back inside.

He was still holding it!

And he had made too much noise. The door of the bottle room began to open. All he could do was hide the bottle in his pocket.

"Oh, I thought everyone had left...."

She was right behind him.

Ben turned, caught in his guilt like a rat in a trap.

"I've seen you before, haven't I?" said Constance Garner-Gee.

Did she see me pocketing that bottle? Ben thought. He needed to answer politely. At a loss for words, he remembered the invitation. He pulled it out and thrust it into her hands.

Her eyes shot open. "Who gave this to you?"

"I ... I found it."

"But we don't send these out anymore. I haven't seen one in years. Where did you get it?"

"It came with the milk."

"The milk?"

"It was in an envelope behind the milk bottles."

She frowned.

"It really was," he insisted.

"Really?" she said, dryly suspicious. "That's very odd indeed. I don't charge children admission, so you didn't need an invitation. But seeing as you have one, perhaps I should show you around until your mother comes for you. Don't worry — we're closing for the day soon, but I won't lock the front door yet. You don't want to stay in here anyway, do you?" She wrinkled her nose. "It's a musty little room, I always think."

Ben followed her out. His chest felt tight and weak with dread because he didn't know how much she had seen.

Did she think he was a thief?

Might she phone the police?

Or Mom?

"Let me show you one of my favorite rooms instead," she said, ushering him into the insect room.

It was the last room Ben would have chosen, but he didn't want to say so; in fact, he was having trouble speaking at all because though he knew he needed to talk, he couldn't think where to start. He began to understand why Mom had found it so difficult to talk about Dad.

The insect room was lined from ceiling to floor with narrow wooden drawers, and some of them were open and none of them were locked. You could pull out any one of them to see a parade of dragonflies, or moths, or hornets, or butterflies, or grasshoppers and wasps, or weevils and beetles. There were more beetles than anything else, in every imaginable color and

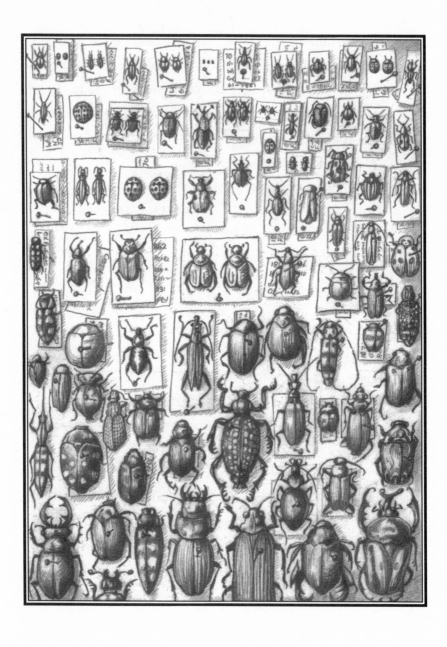

pattern; each one had a tiny handwritten label and was pinned through the thorax to the backboard.

"When I was your age, I used to think they were like knights in heraldic armor," said Constance.

"There's so many," marveled Ben.

"Thousands of them." She opened more drawers so he could see how many were displayed there in orderly rows. "My family collected most of them before I was born."

"That long ago," said Ben — and then he felt awkward because he knew you shouldn't make comments about a lady's age.

Luckily Miss Garner-Gee seemed so amused that Ben decided she couldn't have seen him pocketing the bottle. He was beginning to relax when she said, "I remember where I saw you now. You were here yesterday. Mr. Pike chased you away, didn't he?"

Ben tensed.

"Don't look so frightened," she said. "I expect you found the door open and wandered in because you liked the look of the place. Children are always welcome here. Mr. Pike had no right to chase you away."

Now, as if her kindness had switched on his voice, the words came pouring out of Ben; he felt desperate to explain why he had been trespassing. "Don't trust that Mr. Pike," he said. "He

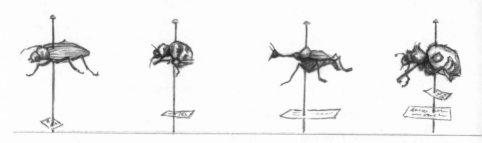

wants to throw me and my mom out of our apartment — and he wants to knock down your museum too. I came to tell you what I heard him saying yesterday." In a great rush he explained what he'd heard in the café, and then he told her about Mom's shop, and how worried they were about their home — and he might have gotten around to mentioning the visit with his dad except that Miss Garner-Gee held up her hand and interrupted him.

"It's very brave of you to come and tell me what you heard," she said gently, "and I can see why you're angry. But are you sure you understood what the grown-ups were saying? This notion of a flood — I can't really believe it."

"I did understand him," said Ben. "Please don't trust him."

She was looking worried now. "It's not as simple as that," she replied.

Ben thought, *Yes, it is*. Tears pricked his eyes, but the explanations dried up in his throat.

She tried again: "The lady who was with him is the director of —"

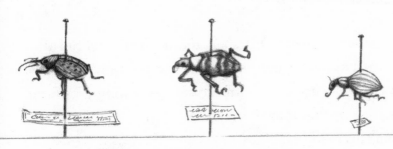

"I know who she is. Don't trust her either."

"I may have to." She smiled sadly. "I do love this museum, you know. I've spent most of my life caring for it, but —"

"So why are you going to sell it to them?" cried Ben. Then he blushed red as a raspberry.

He thought she wouldn't answer. He thought she would be angry and send him packing. To his surprise, she only sighed. "I can see you already love this museum too," she said. "It's a wonderful place, I know, but I can't look after it forever. The city council doesn't have any money to help, and I've failed to trace any of my family. If I had, things might have been different . . . but now it's too late. I must think about what will happen to the museum after I go. There's no one else ready to take it over, but I'd like to know the collection will stay in this city. If it goes to Miss Snow at the Discovery Museum, then children like you will be able to visit it. Wouldn't that be better than having the collection split up and sent all over the country?"

"No," Ben said stubbornly. "I think it should stay here." And he wanted to say so much more, wanted to ask her about all sorts of things — about Dad, about the idea he was formulating about the blue stone, but he couldn't find the words. Besides, he knew that what she said made sense — boring grown-up sense, the sort that ruined everything. He hung his head.

"Come and look at my bees," she said, leading him over to the crystal hive, which stood against the window.

"I think they delivered the invitation to my house," he mumbled.

"That's not very likely, is it?" Constance replied. Then she invited him to climb the hive steps to take a closer look.

It seemed rude to refuse.

A Speckle of Life

CHAPTER 18

The crystal hive had been designed so you could watch the bees working inside. Ben saw hundreds of them, tightly packed and quivering, on row upon row of hexagonal wax cells. He thought it looked almost like a miniature apartment building; indeed, the hive even had its own busy road to the outside — a curved glass tunnel built into the window, fashioned so that the bees could fly outside and forage for food. He watched them traveling back and forth down the tunnel. Some of them were carrying pollen from early-flowering bushes. Others were on some unknown business. None of them paid him any attention.

"Is there anything else here that's alive?" he blurted out. Then he felt embarrassed because it was such a childish question.

To his surprise, Constance Garner-Gee didn't laugh. She only said vaguely, "Well, there are a lot of exhibits that look lifelike."

"Like the owl," he mumbled.

"There are several owls here."

139

"There was an owl in the lobby yesterday that wasn't there today."

"You saw the scops owl in the lobby?" She glanced at him sharply now.

He nodded nervously.

"No. You couldn't have. You must be confused about where you saw it. The scops owl is in the atrium. Though I agree, that owl is a bit special—or so I used to think when I was your age. Mind you, if you look hard in any museum, I expect you'll find a few objects that seem to have a bit more spirit than the rest. Almost as if—well, yes—as if they have a speckle of life about them." She smiled then, a crooked smile as if she were mocking herself, and added, "Maybe they're a bit haunted by the thoughts and fingerprints of the people who once loved them."

"Haunted?" said Ben. He looked back at the insects pinned in their drawers. "You mean . . . like ghosts?"

"Oh, I never think of it like that."

"Like what, then?"

"That's tricky to explain," she mused. "Goodness, I haven't thought about this for ever so long, but I used to wonder if it's because they were particularly special to someone once. I think those special ones are often a bit more grimy and worn — from being handled maybe—or sometimes they're shiny with

140

use. Perhaps the craftsman who created them didn't want to part with them because he thought he'd made something particularly fine. Or maybe after they were found, they became a much-loved treasure, or they were discovered after a lifetime of searching. That scops owl was my uncle Hector's favorite specimen when he was a boy; he even gave it a name — he used to call it Flummery. And my grandfather was particularly fond of the pygmy hippo at the end of the hallway. Do you know the animal I mean?"

Ben nodded.

"My grandfather brought it here just before he died. My grandmother told me he had been searching for it for a long time."

"How long?" Ben asked.

Constance didn't answer. She sniffed and looked around, as if she'd caught the scent of something odd. Ben fancied that the nearest bees in the hive had changed their dance too, and though at first it was a tiny change, a ripple swept across the colony until they all danced more vigorously.

"They look like they're upset about something," said Ben, backing down the steps.

"Possibly," she replied. "Bees are very intelligent, and I think they might be telling us there's going to be a most enormous thunderstorm. Can you smell the ozone?"

"A bit," said Ben. He could smell something odd. But to him

it didn't smell quite like a thunderstorm. It was a faintly gluey scent, and it worried him. It reminded him of the smell when he had first opened the silver bottle.

"When is your mother meeting you?"

"She's not," he said. "I'm allowed to bike home on my own."

"Really? Then perhaps you should wait a little longer so you're not caught in the storm. It's very odd weather for February — feels quite oppressive. How about we have a cup of tea in my office while we wait for it to pass? I need one after what you've told me."

"Is there a pufferfish lamp in the office?" Ben asked.

She looked astonished. "How on earth did you know that?"

"I ... maybe I dreamed it."

"Would you like to see it?"

Ben nodded.

They left the insect room without troubling to close the drawers, and Constance made him feel more at ease by naming the animals in both English and Latin as they headed up the stairs.

The pufferfish lamp hung before the office window, its dusty spines against the leaden sky.

"Its eyes are shut," said Ben, disappointed.

Constance chuckled. "When I was your age, I imagined it could open them."

"Did you ever think it talked?"

She sighed wistfully. "A long time ago I used to imagine all sorts of things. I don't hear them anymore. Though talking to you makes me wonder when I stopped listening." She shivered and put another log on the glowing embers of the fire. "Goodness, isn't it getting damp and clammy? That thunderstorm smells much closer. Sit down and warm yourself while I brew some tea. I expect you'd like some toast too?"

She departed through a different door, and soon Ben could hear her filling a kettle somewhere quite far off. He hadn't dared to tell her that he didn't like tea, so he worried about drinking it as he waited on the green sofa. Warmth and worry and guilt spread through him: the warmth from the fire made him open his coat; the worry and the guilt, especially when he thought of the silver bottle, made him wriggle. He longed to return it to the table cabinet, but if Miss Garner-Gee hadn't noticed the bottle was missing, he didn't want to draw her attention to it. Anyway,

there was so much he needed to ask her. Most of all he wanted to ask her about Dad.

As he fretted about how to begin, his eyes drifted over the curious objects on the mantelpiece. There was a carved vase holding some twigs with a flying lizard twisted among them, and a bone whistle shaped like a squirrel. A cigar box full of dead butterflies stood open next to a hummingbird's nest and a tiny glass box containing two seahorses snuggled together in cotton batting. In the center of the shelf was a perfectly formed glass apple. It was fashioned so beautifully that at first he thought it was real. Then he realized that it glowed slightly. This was because of the light that refracted through the glass, but Ben felt like he could see the soul of a real apple. As he put out his hand to touch it, a dull metal dial shaped a little like a ship caught his eye.

"That's on the ticket," he murmured.

"It's called the Little Ship of Venice," said a crackly paper-ish voice from behind him.

Ben snatched his hand back.

"Fundamentally flawed, Humphrey always said," the voice added. "But when Constance was your age, she believed it had magical properties, and even now it's a personal favorite of hers. I sometimes hear her saying she'd like to sail away in it."

By this point Ben was twisting around anxiously. *The problem with talking objects,* he thought, *is that you never quite know which one is speaking.* He knew the old lady was still in the other room, so it definitely couldn't be her. However, that left . . . everything else in the room. He was relieved when he noticed that the pufferfish was glowing under its layer of dust. It saved on guessing time.

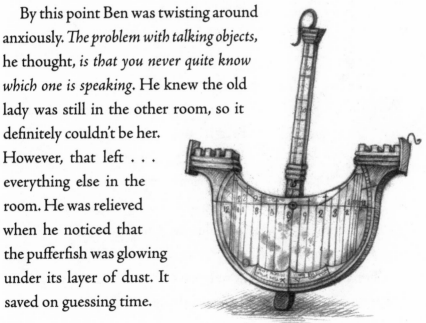

The Pufferfish

CHAPTER 19

"You've grown since I last saw you," the pufferfish said. "Let's see . . . how old would you have been?"

"I'm small for my age," Ben said gruffly.

"But big enough to warn Constance what those people are up to. I do hope you *have* warned her?" Its round eyes were open now, and it watched him critically.

"Couldn't you have warned her yourself?" said Ben sullenly.

The pufferfish deflated as it let out its breath. "Believe me, I've tried to talk to her until I've almost blown a spike. She hasn't been receptive to my comments since she was your age. Do you see those papers below me on the desk?"

Ben nodded.

"For more than a hundred years I've been casting light on papers, but those are the most dangerous I've ever seen." It

146

began to swing on its chain as it explained. "They're the plans for moving the Gee collection to a new building. There's even a drawing. Look: it shows the annex that the Pike man is proposing to build onto the Discovery Museum. Frankly, it won't be roomy. Tara Snow will dispose of most of us if she moves the collection there. And look at me. Do you think I'll be welcome in her stylish new museum?"

Ben didn't know how to answer. The pufferfish lamp was dusty and cracked, and many of its prickles had snapped right off. It looked worn and scruffy.

Now it took a deep breath so that it expanded into a tight round ball, and its voice eked out with a whistle as it said, "I've been hanging here in front of this window since the beginning of the Gee Museum. See that muddy building site out there? A fine line of houses used to stand where they've built those ugly brick boxes. I watched those machines pull the old homes down. Before that I watched yellow bins filling with what nobody wanted. How much

longer before the yellow bins
arrive at the doors of the Gee
Museum and are filled up
with what Tara Snow doesn't
want? How many of us will
survive? Will anyone want an
old pufferfish lamp?"

"I would," declared
Ben. "And I don't
think Miss Garner-
Gee will ever let any
of you end up in a
bin. She said today
that she loved the
museum."

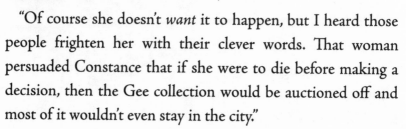

"Of course she doesn't *want* it to happen, but I heard those
people frighten her with their clever words. That woman
persuaded Constance that if she were to die before making a
decision, then the Gee collection would be auctioned off and
most of it wouldn't even stay in the city."

"Is that true?"

"Perhaps it is — *if* Constance dies without deciding what to
do. The trouble is, she's almost given up, poor old trout. She
thinks there's no one left who cares about the museum."

"*I* care," said Ben.

"Do you?" rattled the pufferfish, swinging harder. "But how much? That's the thorny question. Certainly you'll need some hard proof before you take any action — and I suppose that's understandable."

"Proof? What d'you mean?"

"I mean that I can point you to some proof. *Something in print is always best,* so Humphrey used to say. Can you see that newspaper clipping on the mantelpiece? Over there, behind the Little Ship of Venice. Take it! Be sharp now. She'll be back any minute."

"But that's stealing," protested Ben.

"Borrow it, then," the pufferfish said. "Have you no spine, boy? At least read it, and tell your mother all about it."

"I suppose I could...."

"Hurry!" begged the pufferfish. "Something is wrong this afternoon: by the pricking of my spikes, I sense more than a storm approaching."

Ben reached for the newspaper clipping: it was rolled and old and yellowed with age, and when he unfolded the brittle paper, his eyes and mouth grew round. He was looking at a photo of a boat, and standing in front of it was a young couple with a very small boy. The young woman in the picture was definitely his mom.

LOST AT SEA

It is with great sadness that we report the discovery of the wreck of a small vessel off the coast of Sulawesi. The wreck is believed to be the remains of the *Sea Witch*, the boat captained by the adventurer Simon Garner-Gee who was on a return voyage to Micronesia with his young family (pictured). Radio contact with the vessel ceased on the 12th of February during a typhoon. Sadly there have been no further reports and they are now believed to be lost at sea.

"But me and Mom never went," said Ben.

"Constance thought that you did. She lost another part of her heart when she saw that newspaper and thought that you had all died. To be sure, the bees knew otherwise, because a posse of them went to see the boat off, so they knew you weren't on it. They combed the town until they found you, alive and living under a false name. And since then we have waited for you to grow up strong and —"

"I wasn't living under a false name," protested Ben. "I have the same name as my mom."

"You are a Gee too. Surely you felt it as soon as you stepped into the museum. Doesn't the museum speak to you? I think that is because it is yours — yours or no one's — and soon it will be no one's, because it will no longer exist. Even tended by the bees' food, Constance has been unable to do more than trust to fate. Now she has lost hope altogether. And who can blame her, running this place on her own at her age? She's too old to master all the modern technology needed nowadays. Yet we believe she could still learn if she had some help, and some reason to think the museum has a future. And here you are now. You're our last hope. Thank goodness you didn't listen to Leon and open that bottle. I knew you wouldn't do anything so spineless if you could see some real proof."

Ben stared down at the newspaper. He wished he could

explain what had happened with the bottle, but at that very instant they heard the old lady returning.

"Quick, pocket it. She's coming!" wheezed the pufferfish.

So Ben stuffed the newspaper clipping into his pocket, with the bottle, and felt doubly guilty. When Constance Garner-Gee came in with the tea tray, he was back on the green sofa, though his ears were burning so much that he feared they must look like two slices of beet on the sides of his head.

Teatime and Bee-Time

CHAPTER 20

There were two china honeypots on the tea tray: a small one and a large one.

Constance offered the larger one to Ben.

Ben was hungry. His mouth watered as he lifted the lid and spread a greedy helping of honey on his toast.

Constance spooned some beige paste from the smaller pot into her own tea. "I won't offer you any of this," she explained. "It's royal jelly. The bees make it to feed to their queens. It tastes really rather disgusting, but it does make me feel younger. I believe it's kept me going all these years. You stick to the honey, though. You're young and full of life. Don't you think our bees make delicious honey?"

"Yumsh." Ben had his mouth full.

"I'm glad you agree. Now, where were we?" she said. "You were warning me about Mr. Pike, weren't you? And you had

153

some strange ideas about a flood, and you were going to tell me where you really got that invitation."

Now the toast and honey felt like cardboard in Ben's mouth. "I told you the truth," he protested. "The invitation *did* come with the milk, and the sengi said—"

"The sengi?"

"It's a shrew thing in the—"

"Yes, I know. It's in the African small animal cabinet." Tea slopped into her saucer as her hand shook. "That shrew was my grandmother's favorite exhibit."

"Well, it can speak," said Ben stoutly. "It's another of the special things, isn't it? I think there's something magic about them."

Constance was very still. "I used to think so," she said faintly.

"Then . . . why not now?" said Ben. "Because grown-ups don't believe in magic?"

There was an awkward pause.

"It's hard to believe in magic when you grow up," she said, sweeping her hand over her chin. "Mind you, my grandfather did. Just before he died, he told me there was a magical beast and a hidden treasure here, which would protect the museum and everyone in it."

"What sort of treasure?"

154

"He wouldn't tell me that because he thought my uncles would fight over it — and they probably would have. They fought over everything after he died. I think my grandmother knew something about it, though. She raised me after my mother died. She told me the treasure was a beautiful blue jewel and that it belonged to a watercow."

"Didn't you ever look for it?"

"Well, of course I did. We all did. It could have had some value. But there's no water buffalo in this museum and no blue jewel that we ever found. It was about then that my uncles began to argue among themselves. Eventually Montgomery, my favorite uncle — and perhaps my grandmother's favorite too — moved far away to the other side of the world. He never came back. My grandmother died not long afterward, and I had to go away to school. And you know, it's very hard to believe in magic and luck when people die and your world turns upside down."

"Didn't you ever look to see if your grandmother had it?"

"Of course I did," she said. "I have all her jewelry. There wasn't much. Nothing of value. Nothing blue. And truthfully I don't care much about stones and jewels. People and animals are more important to me."

"What if Montgomery found it and took it when he went away?"

She looked startled. "D'you know, I'd never thought of that."

Ben took a deep breath. If he ever was going to say it, now was the time. "My dad had a blue stone. He's dead now, but he left it for me. I think you met my dad once, when I was little. I remember it because he brought me here and I met you too."

Constance had gone very pale and was staring at him. "What's your name?" she said quietly.

"Ben," he said. Thinking of Mom, he added, "Ben Makepeace. I've got my mom's name."

Her mouth opened, but now it was she who seemed at a loss for words.

Ben took a savage bite of bread and honey, but as he chewed, he suddenly felt chilled, and a brief sense of hideous wrongness overcame him. It was a really shocking feeling, harsh as a loud sharp discord or a twang of toothache. He thought it was only in his own head until he saw Constance Garner-Gee jump to her feet — exactly as there came a blistering flash and an ear-splitting crack that rattled the windows.

"I don't think that's lightning," cried Constance as an overpowering stench of ozone and sulfur and a strange, gluey smell seeped into the room. And then a thought seemed to strike her and she turned to Ben searchingly. "Oh my goodness," she said. "You were in the bottle room. You opened that silver bottle with the witch in it, didn't you?"

He nodded. There was no point in pretending. The air around them began to tremble and pulse with a note like the sound of a wet finger circling the rim of a glass. But it grew louder than that — and then louder still, until the glass apple on the mantelpiece split with a loud crack, clean down the middle. It lay in two halves, wobbling.

In the ominous quiet that followed, Ben reached out and tried to put the two halves back together. He knew it was useless, but he wished he could put something right.

"Don't worry about it," said Constance. "Sometimes when things break, it sets us free to move on."

"You said you didn't believe in magic."

"I think I taught myself not to."

"But you have to accept help exists before it can be of much use," said the pufferfish.

This time when the pufferfish spoke, Constance turned to gaze at it with a strange mixture of delight and fear in her face. And Ben knew she had heard it too, for she answered fervently, "I'll accept whatever help I can get from now on. Let's hope I haven't left it too late."

She crossed the room and pulled the door open, and they saw that the atrium was transformed. It was wreathed with smoke — or perhaps it was mist, for the air felt wet, as though a rogue cloud had invaded the museum. From within the mist there came the sound of humming. The humming grew louder, and soon they saw that the mist had a blacker, writhing center of thoroughly excited bees.

"Well, this seems like a challenge if ever there was one," said Constance. "I suppose there could still be a logical explanation, but it doesn't seem likely."

The pufferfish swung on its chain. "Only a grown-up could think for a moment that this wasn't caused by magic," it said mildly.

Ben glanced back at it and noticed that Constance had left her cane by the fireside. He was about to fetch it for her, but the pufferfish said, "Leave it. She'll come and retrieve it herself if she needs it."

The Mist

CHAPTER 21

There was no time for more questions or explanations. The old lady's gray eyes were pinned on Ben. "Listen," she said urgently. "I want you to go home *now*. No, don't argue, I need to know that you're safe. I don't understand why the bees are swarming — I'm not sure what is happening at all — but I do know my bees, and they behave more calmly when there are no strangers around. I want you to quietly follow me downstairs and then *leave* by the back door, while I

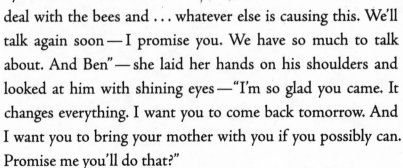

deal with the bees and . . . whatever else is causing this. We'll talk again soon — I promise you. We have so much to talk about. And Ben" — she laid her hands on his shoulders and looked at him with shining eyes — "I'm so glad you came. It changes everything. I want you to come back tomorrow. And I want you to bring your mother with you if you possibly can. Promise me you'll do that?"

159

He mumbled, "I promise." Then he said, "Where is the back door? I didn't see one."

"It's under the gallery, to the right of the stairs. Go behind the giraffes." Constance put an arm around him. "And now you must keep very, very still because . . ."

Her voice trailed off, for at that moment the bees surged forward, surrounding them both in a black heaving chaos that Ben couldn't bear. He pulled away from her and cowered in panic against the glass museum cabinets with his hands up to his face, waiting to be stung, sure he'd be stung many times, maybe stung until he was dead.

Yet as the turmoil swept around him, he felt no more than moist air ripple against his flesh. Only one bee collided with him — and it didn't sting — and just as quickly, they all moved on to engulf Constance. They covered her like a second skin. Ben was horrified. How could she remain calm with bees crawling all over her? Some of them were in her hair. He gathered himself to shout, to save her, to do something, but then the shout died in his throat — because she was smiling.

She called to him, "You see! They mean no harm."

And Ben saw that her cheeks had a hint of pink, and she looked happy. It occurred to him that the bees had swarmed to fetch her. And that she was content to be fetched.

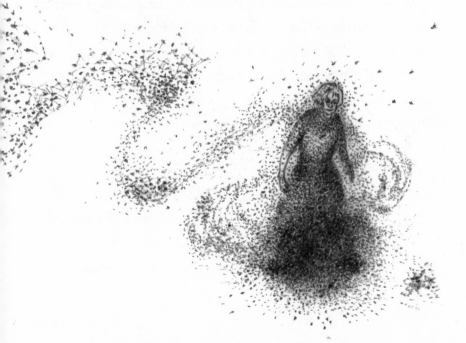

"I think the bees know you, Ben," she cried. "They know you're one of the family. Don't look so worried. This swarm is something I can handle."

"This is all because I opened the bottle, isn't it?" wailed Ben, staring wide-eyed at the bees and the mist.

"It . . . well, perhaps it is — but, Ben, if there is a witch, or something like it, then it's been here for a very long time and it's a part of this place." She turned and waved a bee-enrobed arm as she began to descend the stairs. "*Promise* you'll come back tomorrow?"

"I will," he assured her.

Even so, he couldn't bear to follow her down the stairs. He told himself he might disturb the bees and make things worse if he caught up to her. That was what he told himself, but actually, he was too afraid to approach them. Instead, he leaned over the top of the balustrade, peering into the enfolding whiteness, watching. And, to his surprise, he identified the gray bulk of the hippo waiting at the foot of the stairs.

Constance greeted the hippo like a long-lost friend. Hands on either side of his face, she paused to say something that Ben couldn't hear, though he was pretty sure that the hippo was saying something back to her. A moment later, she used the stairs as a mounting block in order to climb onto his broad back and they moved away, carrying the swarm with them. Ben had time to notice that her feet did not quite reach the ground before the mist dropped like a white curtain and they vanished.

Alone in the swirling haze, Ben felt his dread of the witch's malice return double-fold. He fumbled along the balustrade, unable to see, though he stretched his eyes so wide that his cheeks and temples ached.

Here were the stairs, slippery and wet; he took one step, two steps, three. He glimpsed the giraffes, still on the left of the stairs, but visible only from the neck up so that they appeared to float on the mist like a two-headed sea serpent. He didn't like that, so he lurched away to the other side, only to be confronted by the dinosaur skeleton: its ancient skull was entwined in tendrils of mist, which hid, then revealed, then hid its blind eye sockets and billowed like smoke through its jaws.

Like dragon's breath, Ben thought.

Then he lost his nerve altogether and ran. With his mind full of witches and where they might be, he fled down the stairs, bolting in the direction of the back door — or the place where the back door ought to have been. Other animals in the atrium loomed through the mist, appearing like ghostly statues in an ornamental pool. Yet it was as if there were no edges to the room. And he had a creeping sense that something in the mist was searching for him, reaching to find him before he found the door.

Ben forced himself to halt.

He noticed that the mist had gathered on the floor as if it were heavier than air. It made the ground beneath glimmer with a strange sheen, like liquid pearl. He could hardly see his feet.

He listened.

He heard the steady drip of water, and a buzzing, which was probably the bees, but there were other sounds too: small scufflings and scratchings, a ghostly flapping that seemed to be moving nearer. Ben wondered what sort of sounds a witch would make, and though he tried to be silent, the pounding of his own heart filled his ears so that he couldn't tell whether he was hearing wings or his own breathing.

Then something struck him — hard.

Through the Fog and Filthy Air

CHAPTER 22

Ben was knocked clean off his feet. He fell awkwardly, bashing his knee when he hit the floor. Covering his head with his hands, he whimpered in terror as the nightmare thing, whatever it was, flapped and wriggled over his back.

Then it spoke: "So clumsy!" it squeaked. "I hope you haven't broken him."

Ben lifted his head.

The larger part of the thing — which turned out to be Flummery the owl — fluttered off his back and onto the floor.

"You're all right, boy, aren't you?" said Flummery, peering into Ben's face. "Dear, oh dear, I thought you'd hold your ground."

Ben sat up.

The sengi popped out from behind the owl's head. "Ben didn't expect you to land on him," she scolded as she sprang to the ground. Then, without any warning, she leaped onto Ben's injured knee. "Last time I accept a ride from that owl," she announced.

165

After that she whisked up to Ben's breast pocket, pushed her nose into it as if she was checking it out, then somersaulted inside, flicking him smartly on the chin with her tail as she went. "That's better," she said. Her wriggling nose poked over the edge of his pocket.

"Help yourself," muttered Ben, rubbing his knee.

"Well, it's good we found you. Some fool has opened that silver bottle and let the witch out, so now —"

"But you and Leon *told* me to open it!"

Both creatures stared. "So it *was* you," said the sengi.

Ben glared at the sengi resentfully — whereupon she became very busy squeezing the mist from her whiskers and muttered, "I admit I had a *small* part in advising you to open it. I was *possibly* mistaken."

"Possibly!" Flummery squawked.

"Leon showed me where it was," said Ben.

"So that explains why he's gone into hiding," the sengi spat. She bristled to twice her normal size and cursed in an undertone, "Cross-eyed mazzard, he ought to be ashamed of himself."

"Mind your tongue," hissed the owl, nodding toward Ben.

But Ben was busy watching the mist twining around them, swirling and stretching like a growing being. "Did the witch make this mist?" he asked in a low voice.

Flummery blinked. "Don't you recognize wild magic when you see it?" he said.

"I don't know anything about wild magic!" said Ben. "But I'm guessing it's a bad witch."

"Well — possibly," twittered Flummery. "Though it could be that she's just feeling grumpy. We ought to hope for the best."

"There isn't any best," snapped the sengi. "If you ask me, she's as bitter as an oak apple and just about as nasty."

"She does *seem* pretty unfriendly," Flummery admitted. "And with small unfriendly witches, there's often wild magic and odd weather — like this mist. We ought to expect some space-changing too."

"What d'you mean?" said Ben.

"Well, wild magic carries memories of other places it has inhabited. That means it can distort our perception of any space it fills."

Ben was confused. "Wait — are you saying wild magic can make a place seem like it's a different shape?"

"Exactly. And that explains why this room feels so much bigger."

"No wonder I got lost."

"Yes, and it may keep changing yet," fretted the sengi. "But that's the least of it."

"There could be other unfortunate side effects," the owl

agreed. "Before too long, some of the exhibits *might* begin to be a little more lively."

"What d'you mean?" Ben was aghast.

The owl folded his wings behind his back and began to strut like a schoolteacher. "Think about this mist," he said. "It's not natural, is it? In fact, it's supernatural, so it adds a bit of supernatural fizz to anything it penetrates — not immediately, or we'd really be in trouble, but when it's had time to soak into everything . . . well —"

"Some of these creatures might remember how they used to move around," said the sengi bluntly.

"They might," said the owl. "But don't worry: it'll only be the small creatures at first. The insects are beginning to stir now. That's because they can absorb more mist as a percentage of their size, if you're interested in how it happens —"

"We're not," squeaked the sengi.

"Well, you should be," said the owl. "It's very important. It means our immediate problem will be controlling the smallest exhibits, and the bees will attend to that." He paused and closed his eyes for a moment, as if he was thinking hard. Then he said, "This explains why the hive was roused. Some of the bugs in the insect room collection are tiny. They must have stirred almost at once. I expect most of the bees are busy herding them back. They'll have more trouble with the larger exhibits, but we needn't worry about lions for at least an hour or two. Hopefully by then Constance and the hippo will have dealt with the witch."

The sengi was gnawing at her tail again. "But even if they do, will that stop the wild magic?" she said worriedly. "I've heard that once it's been summoned, even its creator can't do much to control it."

Ben was appalled. "It's my fault, isn't it?" he said. "If I'd listened to you ..."

"Nonsense — it could have happened to anyone," said Flummery kindly. "Beak up, boy. There's a good side to this. Constance is working with us again; after meeting you, she seems to be able to hear us as she used to. It could be because of the magic in the air, but if you ask me, it's because you restored her faith in the museum."

"She's in the fish room tackling the witch right now," said the sengi. "We met on the way, and she sent us to make sure you went straight home."

"But what if I could help?" said Ben. He took a deep breath, because he felt scared of what he was going to suggest. "Look, I've still got the bottle. What if I catch the witch and put her back in it?"

The other two glanced at each other.

"I'm not sure that would work," said the sengi.

"Wouldn't be easy," said Flummery. He took a hop-jump-flutter that carried him with a *flop* onto Ben's shoulder. "But I'd think you were a very brave boy if you tried."

When an owl lands on your shoulder, it can feel like a cheerful thump on the back from a very large man. And Flummery's scaly yellow toes gripped so tight that his talons prickled all the way through Ben's coat. His feathers smelled slightly moldy too and his squawking, so close up, was uncomfortably shrill. Yet though Ben was startled and shaken, he felt at the same time rather honored, because Flummery was a lovely owl.

"I definitely want to try," he said, and he stood up very carefully so as not to dislodge his passengers. "Which way?"

"That's easy," said the sengi, gyrating her nose. "They're in the fish room — first room down the hall, on the left, over there."

Ben peered into the whiteness. "How can you tell? I can't see anything."

"Can't you smell them? That's how we found you."

Ben could only smell the odd gluey scent of the mist. "You'll have to direct me," he said as he walked.

Presently they reached the steps that marked the edge of the sunken court. Beyond was an area of thicker mist that looked intensely secret. Yet this was where they headed because it hid the entrance to the hallway. Beads of mist like tiny pearls gathered on the sengi's fur as she guided them. Ben felt mist in his own hair too, and in Flummery's feathers as they brushed his cheek, while all around them the sinister whiteness blurred their whereabouts. Nevertheless, it concealed them too, and that was good because soon Ben could hear Constance Garner-Gee and the hippo speaking close by.

But they weren't alone. There was another voice too, a voice so iced with spite that chills shivered all along Ben's spine. He didn't doubt that he was hearing the witch.

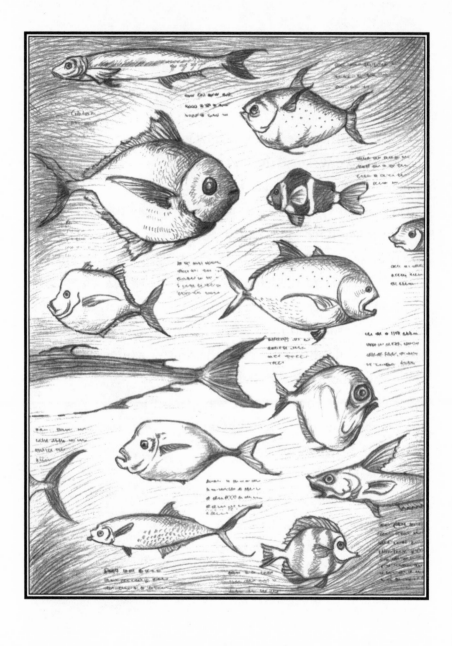

Spite and Malice in the Fish Room

CHAPTER 23

Ben hesitated on the threshold. He hoped that the mist would hide him as he tried to peer inside. Obviously that meant he couldn't see much either; the mist blurred the room, flexing and undulating in waves so that the fish in their towering cabinets — salmon and carp, pompanos and stingrays — appeared to swim along the walls. All the same, he soon located the moving bulk that was Constance and the hippo. They were backed up into the far corner of the room.

At first the witch was harder to spot, because she was tiny and dressed in knitted cobwebs that blended with the color of the mist. Only her hair betrayed her, as it was the color and shape of rusted bedsprings, and as she flew past, there was a flash of metallic green. This was because she was riding on a handsome green beetle, which buzzed back and forth in a triangle like a bothersome fly. As they flew, the witch steamed gently: vapor issued from her nose and ears — it was the source of the mist.

173

Constance was trying to reason with her. "The Gees didn't capture you at all," she was pleading. "That bottle was already sealed when my uncle Montgomery bought it from another collector."

"How would you like to be collected?" whined the witch. She had a high-pitched voice, scratchy as fingernails on a chalkboard.

"I wouldn't like it at all," said Constance. "But it was such a long time ago."

"I *know* how long. Wasn't I trapped in that blasted bottle for every second of it?"

"I'm sorry! I told you I'm sorry, but I didn't know you were in there — nobody did. Nobody here ever meant to be cruel, especially not Uncle Montgomery."

"That's for me to decide."

"But it's *true:* he began to collect curiosities because he was having doubts about collecting wild creatures. The silver bottle was part of all that. I remember when it arrived here — I was a child and it frightened me, although Montgomery assured me there was nothing inside it."

"A bag of lies. *He* wrote the label."

"He did write the label. But it was a record

of what he'd heard from
someone else. He was
interested in superstitions
and curiosities — and he
thought that our visitors
would be too."

"So I'm only a curiosity?" fumed
the witch. "How about you? *You* could have let me out years
ago instead of robbing me of my youth and beauty. Would you
like to be stuck in a bottle?"

"Of course I wouldn't," Constance
said hastily. "And I ought to
have done something earlier.
But the bottle always made me
uncomfortable, so I stayed away from
it. I've already told you how sorry I am
about that — but heavens to goodness, you're free now, so what
more do you want of us?"

There was a pause. Then the witch's reply came harsh and
sudden as a cat's hiss: "I'm not interested in goodness after
ninety years a-stewing in a bottle."

"What about the boy? Don't you owe him anything? He set
you free. Think about him before you act. He's —"

"I'd rather think about revenge," said the witch in a voice that

oozed with poison. And she raised her hands and spread her fingers at Constance in what could have been a spell-casting manner.

Ben felt about as confident as a crumb of cheese in a mousetrap, but he had to do something. He uncorked the silver bottle, stepped into the room, and said, "In that case, you'll have to go back inside this!" (Though quite how he would make that happen he had no idea.)

"Ben, I told you to go home!" gasped Constance, and the hippo stamped in alarm. But Ben was staring at the bottle, which was growing hot in his hand. Out of the blue, it gave a twisted little tug — like the sensation when you switch on a vacuum — and he could see the force of some magic acting on the witch, dragging at her hair, puckering her skin.

The witch looked terrified. Ben was horrified as well; he didn't want to use magic at all, certainly not magic that could harm anyone — even this witch. In fact, it seemed to him that she had some right to feel aggrieved.

Anyway, he needn't have worried, because that was all the bottle did. It wasn't long before everyone guessed that nothing more was going to happen and the witch began to snigger with contempt. "There's words that goes along with that bottle, and you don't know them," she said. "I wish you no ill, boy, but you're not putting me back in there."

She swayed on the beetle's back; then, without warning, she snapped the fingers of both hands straight at the place where Ben stood. And the mist around him began to transform.

It grew more solid, like a wall of warm snow. It seemed to gather and then condense into something thicker. The fumes increased too; their sour, gluey scent became so pungent that it made him feel giddy.

"Steady now," hooted Flummery. "She's blocking us off from Constance."

The owl was right; they couldn't even hear what the witch was saying anymore.

"I've got to get to Constance," cried Ben. Yet he could hardly move forward.

"Cup your hands like you're digging a burrow," said the sengi. She demonstrated with her paws. Ben put the bottle back in his pocket so that he had both hands free. Then he tried making a motion with cupped hands, imitating the sengi, and this way he discovered he could slowly push his way through the mist.

Unfortunately the witch looked up and saw them approaching. With another click of her fingers, the mist grew even thicker until it was almost the consistency of cotton candy; floating strands of it separated, coating them like monster cobwebs, binding Ben's arms to his sides so that he could no longer burrow. He forced his legs to move forward only with extreme effort. Yet he kept them moving all the same, for he didn't want them bound solid like his arms.

"Everyone had better keep their mouths sealed," squeaked the sengi.

"And head for the wall," squawked the owl. "So we can find our way."

Ben shut his lips tight, and he squinted to keep the foul stuff from his eyes, though he felt layers of it floating and settling on his lashes and cheeks. So he closed his eyes altogether, but this was a mistake because within seconds his eyes were sealed shut. He tried taking shallow breaths, but he could feel the fibers invading his nose, and the stench of the fumes grew so stifling that his chest burned and he tasted a flavor of bile and ash.

He might have panicked entirely if he hadn't felt so determined to reach Constance. After all, she was his relative—a distant one, anyway—and he had just found her and he wasn't going to lose her now. This thought drove him forward in a slow, exhausting shuffle, so although they ought to have been trapped like flies in a spider's pantry, he eventually made contact with the wall.

After that, his progress improved because there was a surface to push against. And so he took a few more steps until he felt a hideous scratching and stretching and tugging around his hairline.

He halted in alarm.

He couldn't use his hands to discover what it was, because his arms were all bound up. He thought he was about to scream when a quiet voice hissed, "Keep silent if you don't want her to hear you."

It was the chameleon's voice. Naturally Ben was wary. But almost at once a skein of the fiber was tugged clean away from his face, and he felt damp air against his cheeks. He could breathe properly again. He could move freely. He could open his eyes and see that although the mist surrounding them remained opaque and white, its density had returned to a state resembling vapor. They had broken through the barrier!

Immediately ahead, Leon leaned from a picture frame. He

was shredding a massive sheet of the cotton-candy mist between his claws. It was plain that he had tugged it off them — had rescued them, in fact. All that remained was to destroy the rest, and that didn't take as long as you might expect, because now Ben had his hands free, and the others used their claws and beaks and teeth. The separated filaments of sticky mist, once so strong, now disintegrated like a broken spiderweb.

"Sorry if I scared you," Leon whispered, "but I assumed you'd prefer to breathe."

He didn't look sorry at all. In fact, Ben thought the chameleon looked rather smug. Yet he thanked him, because he was grateful and because it would have been churlish not to. Unfortunately Leon took this as permission to climb onto Ben's other shoulder.

"This time I'll come along and help," he said. "I'll stop you from doing anything too stupid."

Ben thought this was awfully presumptuous, but as it turned out, they were going to need all the help they could get.

The witch had spotted them!

And instead of using more mist charms, she attacked Ben herself.

. . . .   180   . . . .

Terms and Compensation

CHAPTER 24

The next few moments were horribly confusing: Flummery swooped after the witch, aiming to knock her from the air with his wings; he carried the sengi on his back; she was lashing her tail and gnashing her teeth; Constance batted and clapped her hands as if she were chasing giant gnats; and the hippo joined the rumpus too — he stamped and opened his jaws in an alarming roar that startled them all yet did little else but add to the chaos. Meanwhile the witch continued to dart after Ben.

She whizzed so close that he felt the flick of the beetle's wing on his cheek, so close that he glimpsed her eyes: they were purple, and he could see that they were full of fear. And as he ducked and swerved, it occurred to him that she might be as scared as he was. He knew that animals and humans are more dangerous when they are frightened. Might this hold true for witches?

"I'm not even holding the bottle — it's back in my pocket," he said.

She lunged at him again. He dodged. But he'd had an idea. "Wait!" he cried. "Would you go away and leave us in peace if we found you an egg?"

"An egg?" said the witch. She swerved midflight, reined in her beetle, and hovered, regarding Ben with something like respect.

Leon had been patiently waiting for just such a moment as this. Out shot his tongue, and in less time than it takes to blink — bull's-eye! — he seized the beetle and the witch, binding them tightly. Either the witch was stunned by the blow or Constance was remarkably quick; she pounced, and the hippo stepped sideways, so Leon and his captives were bundled away before the witch had a chance to react. By the time Ben caught up with them on the other side of the room, the witch was firmly trapped between Constance's fists. Only her face protruded. She looked as sour as an unripe grape.

"If you try any more tricks, I'll crush you," Constance warned.

The witch snarled. "And if you do, I'll turn you all into weevils."

"Hold her tight," said the hippo. "I don't believe she can cast any spells at all without using her hands."

"Are you sure of that?" hissed the witch.

No one was.

Leon (who was comfortably lounging in the cleft between the hippo's shoulders) looked up from toying with the beetle. "I think you should throw them both into the garbage incinerator," he said. He gave the beetle a poke. (It was helplessly spinning on its back.)

"That's spiteful," said the witch. "I was fighting for my freedom."

"Oh, can't we just give her an egg?" pleaded Ben, for though he was wary of the witch, he couldn't help feeling some sympathy too. "You've got lots of eggs here. I expect there'd be one that she'd like, and you could let her have it in return for leaving us in peace."

The witch eyed Ben like a snake. "You're a sharp one."

Constance looked stumped. "An egg?"

"My mom has a story about witches and eggshells."

"I daresay your mother is a wise sort of woman if she knows such things," said the witch.

"You'd be wise to treat Ben better," growled Constance. "He's tried to spare you twice already."

"Well, I might, if you give me an egg."

Constance looked outraged. "You're hardly in a position to bargain."

"But perhaps we could take a look at the eggs," said the hippo mildly. "Couldn't we consider it compensation for false imprisonment — in return for certain terms?"

"After all this, I very much doubt it was *false* imprisonment," retorted Constance. All the same, when the owl and the sengi led the way, she allowed the hippo to carry her into the hallway.

Ben brought up the rear. He was relieved to see that they

were leaving the mist behind. It clung to the atrium end of the hall and around the door to the insect room, and seemed somehow almost as subdued as the witch. By the time they reached the egg room, he could barely see a wisp of it.

The witch surveyed the egg cabinet. Her face was as sharp as a pin as she gazed at the speckled blues and greens of the songbird eggs, and the blotched chestnut-honey of the buzzard egg, and a goshawk's egg the color of the moon. She thrust her nose forward for a better look at a mottled iron-brown egg that had once belonged to an emu. In the end, though, the egg that she chose was the largest of all — the egg of the extinct elephant bird.

"I'll take that," she said, and her eyes gleamed a shade of magenta with greed.

"But that's the best in the collection," protested Constance. "It's very rare."

"So am I," said the witch, "and you can't deny that you owe me compensation."

"Compensation!" Constance huffed — a short disgusted breath. "Before I part with anything, I want your word that no one is to be turned into a weevil and —"

"Done!"

"No. Wait! Let me finish: I want you to promise that Ben will be safe. And I want all this mist to go. And I want my museum back as it was. And —"

The witch interrupted with a wail. "But I can't undo all that. Nobody can undo wild magic. I'll not conjure up any more, but the mist that's here already will have to run its course."

"I'm afraid that may be true," said the owl as he settled on top of the cabinet of eggs.

"But she made it!" protested the sengi.

"If you spill milk, you can't unspill it," said the witch.

"You can clean it up," retorted Constance.

The witch fixed her with an acid look. "I can do a dozen

things that can't be done, but that's not one of them," she declared. "I can't bind the mist. It's wild. It'll follow its own course until it fades."

"Which will be when?"

The witch smirked. "Bright sunlight'll do it."

They all looked at the dismal gray February light from the window.

"But at this time of year, it could be dreary like this for days!" said Constance.

"Do you want me to stay here all of those days, or will you trust me to go?" said the witch. "Give me that egg and I'll be out of here, fast as measles in a sneeze."

"But why on earth should I trust *you?*"

"Trust is a problem for bad people," said the witch with a wink. "But I give you my word. Would you doubt it?"

"Yes."

The hippo turned his head. He looked at Constance steadily. "We should treat her as we'd wish to be treated ourselves," he said.

"Please," Ben begged.

The witch smiled as sweetly as poisoned berries.

Constance rolled her eyes. "Well, I think this is a very bad idea," she said tartly, and she looked very put out indeed. Nevertheless, she dismounted. After that, she unlocked the egg cabinet, allowing the witch and the beetle to enter.

Once inside, the two of them prowled all along the row of eggs. They made their way to the far end, where the egg of the extinct elephant bird was proudly displayed. The egg dwarfed the witch, but she stood on the beetle's back and crooned to her prize as though it were a living being. She ran her hands over every inch of it she could reach, in the manner that a horse dealer might vet a pony. The shell was old and blemished with

cracks, yet it responded to her touch. It grew smoother. It grew paler. Her hands healed the surface flaws until the shell looked younger and stronger, as if it were newly laid.

The witch began to look healthier too. It was as though she drew some strength back from the egg. She remounted the beetle and the two flew widdershins around it, looping once — twice — until during the third loop the witch reached out and drew on the egg with the index finger of her left hand. Where her nail scraped across the shell, a crack formed that ran all around the crown. Like a hatch, the area above swung open to show the inside of the egg. It glowed with a pearly light. Yet it was empty, until the witch and beetle flew into it. Presently the giant eggshell wobbled on its curved base. Then, very slowly, it began to rotate.

Meanwhile, quiet as a cat, Constance shut the cabinet door. She turned the key in the lock. "I don't know what they're up to, but they can't get out so easily now," she said. After that, she folded her arms and frowned down at Ben. "And now I wish you'd go home before there's any more trouble. I did ask you to leave quite a while ago."

Ben would have liked to explain, but just then something unfortunate happened.

They heard the front doors open, and someone walked inside. This was not so very unlikely, since the museum was still open to the public. Someone could have walked in at any time — indeed, it was lucky that no one had until now. Leon scuttled to the floor and disappeared.

The visitor called out, "Hello?"

Only one word, but they all recognized the voice.

It was Tara Snow.

What Became of the Elephant Bird's Egg

CHAPTER 25

"Let me deal with this," whispered Constance, holding a finger to her lips. "And Ben, please do as I ask and leave by the back door. Go right now."

She didn't wait to see if he obeyed her. Instead she hurried off to the lobby.

"But I'd have to go back through that mist," muttered Ben.

"Time we all went," said the witch. She was leaning with crossed arms upon the crooked edge of the shell, turning slowly as the egg rotated. Ben decided she looked guilty. Was she up to something? He wondered what she'd do when she discovered that she was trapped inside the cabinet.

"Ben, I will carry you through the mist," offered the hippo.

This was tempting. But he wasn't ready to leave yet. "First I want to hear what Miss Snow says," he whispered, and he edged nearer the lobby door to listen.

Constance greeted Miss Snow with great calmness. No one

would have guessed from her manner that anything unusual had happened that day.

"Miss Snow," she exclaimed. "What a surprise! You're a little late, I'm afraid — we're about to close."

"Actually, I know it's nearly four o'clock," Tara Snow gushed, "but I just came on the off chance and I'm so glad to catch you. I'd hoped we could have another little chat. I didn't feel I'd quite explained —"

"Oh no, you explained very well, and I understood you perfectly. I read your papers. Very interesting. And I do agree that the museum's future needs careful thought, but —"

"Oh, that's excellent news —"

"No, no, I'm afraid you misunderstand me, Miss Snow. I'm sorry to spoil your plans, but I've decided my museum is definitely *not* for sale."

"Not for sale!"

"Exactly," said Constance firmly. "*Not.*"

There was a silence. Then Tara Snow stuttered, "But . . . have you considered the consequences? You must plan for the future."

"I have plans," said Constance.

"You do?"

"New plans." Constance grew icily polite. "Miss Snow, in spite of my advanced age, I am still able to control my own affairs. I agree that your offer seemed fair, and I gave it fair consideration. However, my sources have informed me a little more about Mr. Pike's plans for the building — and frankly, a little more about *your* plans for the collection. I gather you intended to take rather less of it than your offer suggested. You must surely understand: that changes everything."

"Your sources?" Tara Snow sounded stunned. "What d'you mean? Who?"

As they were talking, a draft from the open front door drifted into the museum. This cold air meandered across the egg room into the hallway, and before too long it met up with the mist. Maybe the mist didn't like the cold, or maybe it did. Maybe the witch was up to more mischief and had summoned it. Certainly something compelled it to creep forward again, so at about this time in the conversation, wisps of mist snaked into the egg room, and Ben watched in horror as they slithered over the floor toward the lobby.

"Hey!" he whispered fiercely to the witch. "You promised you wouldn't make any more mist."

"And I haven't," she said with a shrug. "But I never said it would rest as it was. No one can contain wild magic. It'll evolve in its own way before it disperses."

"But what is its own way?"

The witch winked. "That depends on the memories at large in this building," she said. Whereupon the giant egg began to whirl so swiftly that soon Ben could see only a blur. A moment

later it tilted, and then — in a shrill rush of wind with a whistle in it — egg, witch, and beetle completely vanished.

In the lobby Tara Snow said, "Did you hear a whistle? And look! Isn't that smoke?"

"Gracious!" Constance said, all in a rush. "Smoke, yes, that's what it is. I must have left the kettle on."

"But that's not from a kettle, surely? There's too much of it. And it smells funny. Like some sort of cleaning chemical. Or glue. Perhaps I should help you sort it out?"

"No, I'd really rather you stayed out of there, as we use . . . a special sort of misty smoke for . . . well, for the bees, you know. I expect it's something to do with that. My bees don't like strangers."

Constance may have hoped that the mention of the bees would scare the woman away. It didn't. It made her more suspicious. "So someone else is there," she said. "I thought I heard someone talking." She drew in her breath sharply. "You're not getting these ideas from that boy? I've seen him hanging around. He's a troublemaker, you know. He's not still here, is he?"

Now Ben was ready to be gone, ready and anxious: he scrambled onto the hippo, quick as a gibbon. Mind you, the hippo's hide was so shiny and wide that Ben almost slipped off the other side. Balancing, in short, was tricky. Yet he gripped with his knees until they ached, and when the hippo asked him if he was ready, he said that he was, because although he wasn't sure what the woman might do if she caught him, he didn't want to find out.

Meanwhile Constance was insisting, "Don't be silly, there's no one there at all. The . . . smoke is . . . automatic. Thank you so very much for your concern, but I'd really rather deal with this myself, so if you'll excuse me . . . I shall have to lock up early today."

"But this is a lot of smoke. Too much for bees. Could it be your boiler?"

"The boiler?" said Constance in a raised voice, almost as if she was warning them. "Exactly. Just what I was going to say. It's often troublesome, I must deal with it directly, so if you wouldn't mind . . ."

Ben didn't hear whether Tara Snow minded or not, because that was when the hippo entered the hallway where the mist was stretching and spreading; it smothered the sound of the women's voices. It was changing shape again.

Wild Magic

CHAPTER 26

It was alarming: the hazy light at the end of the hall appeared so far away that Ben had the impression you get when you look down the wrong end of a telescope. Worse, when he glanced behind, thinking to return the way they had come, he only saw more hall stretching in the opposite direction. The exit to the egg room had vanished.

"Best not to look behind," said the hippo, "and try not to be frightened — fear will make the way seem longer."

"I'm not scared," Ben lied, though panic was rising in his throat. "But we're not getting anywhere at all."

The hippo tried to comfort him. "Wild magic is full of visual tricks, but remember, it is transient."

"What's transient?"

"You heard the witch — she said that in time the mist would disappear..."

"In bright sunlight," moaned Ben. "There's not much chance of that today. What if it goes all thick and webby again?"

The hippo sighed. "It is certainly unpredictable. But now

197

that the witch has gone, I think we'll find that the mist has already evolved to a new phase in its development. What it will do next I cannot tell, but try and remember that it is moving toward its own end, just as we are moving toward the end of this hall — even if it hardly seems so. If you are frightened, hold tight around my neck and then you will know that I am here, whatever happens."

This was not exactly reassuring, but Ben gratefully leaned forward until he half lay over the hippo's shoulders. He clasped his arms around that sturdy neck and was comforted for the first time in hours as he rested his chilled cheek against the hippo's hide, which felt like an old newspaper warmed in the sun. As the hippo plodded on, Ben told himself that there was nothing he could do but lie there, so he resolved not to look for the end of the hall — they'd get there soon enough. Instead he allowed his eyes to drift toward the floor. That was when he had another horrible fright.

There were multitudes of insects marching alongside them. The insect collection was on the move, and though the bees were out in force, herding them back, there were too few bees to make an impact on such numbers. More insects spilled out, pouring into any vacant spaces. They oozed from the doorway of the insect room; they trooped up the walls; they rippled overhead on the ceiling, scrabbling along on their spindly legs.

Most of them still had pins in their backs, or labels attached. Ben yelped in fear before he could stop himself.

The hippo only said mildly, "I had hoped Flummery would have warned you that this could happen when the mist soaked into the exhibits."

"He did," said Ben, trying to swallow his terror. "But I didn't expect..."

"Calm yourself. It really is of no great consequence. We have many bigger problems to face."

"Like what?" wailed Ben.

"One thing at a time," said the hippo. "Now hush and let me think."

He fell silent, and Ben had to be content with that — though he wasn't. Gradually, though, as he brooded on the hippo's back, his fear dwindled, because he realized that the insects really weren't bothering him. Not one of them bit him, or nipped him, or stung; neither did a single one crawl over to inspect him. In fact, they didn't seem conscious of him at all; rather, they moved like sleepwalkers. Once he understood this, he felt able to watch them without feeling so revolted.

"It's true that some of them were once ruthless hunters," remarked the hippo as if he could read Ben's thoughts. "Yet they only preyed on what they needed to eat. Most of our collection would run from you in the wild if they could. Remember that, Ben. Only humans plot wickedness or seek revenge. The biggest dangers you will ever face are likely to come from your own kind."

"You mean Miss Snow?" Ben was alarmed. "But we've left Constance with her."

The hippo sighed. "It's unfortunate Miss Snow entered during open hours. At any other time Leon would have prevented her. But Flummery and the sengi are with Constance now, and Leon will attend to the doors. My concerns are for you. That woman is ruthless when it comes to what she desires. Stay well clear of her."

"I will," said Ben with feeling. "But don't you think she might give up now?"

"It's possible, I suppose," said the hippo doubtfully.

Presently Ben noticed that there were no more doors and the floor ahead had morphed from wooden boards into tiles like the kind in the sunken courtyard. Strangely the hallway still appeared to stretch into the distance, yet they had arrived at four steps like those in the atrium. The hippo slowed to descend these. As Ben leaned back to keep his wobbly seat, he saw that the ceiling had moved. It was farther away, and he could see the sky through it. The walls had altered too. He couldn't say when they had changed, but now instead of brick and plaster, the walls seemed formed of slices of mist, solid as bread, and these stood at attention, holding back whatever was behind them.

He realized then that they were crossing the atrium. But it had changed shape again, just as the owl had said it might. And there was something behind those walls of mist, something that was crashing around. There was more than one of whatever it was, for the thumps and scrapes came from several directions. They were wild sounds and they grew still wilder. And if Ben had been frightened before, it was nothing to how he felt now, especially when he noticed that the insects were disappearing. They seemed to diffuse into the walls, like drops of water on snow. But if they could climb through, then what might climb back the other way?

"Here is the rear door," said the hippo.

And there it was, straight ahead. It was an old metal door, with rusting gray paint and a heavy, ancient bolt. It looked like a door to the outside. The hippo halted and Ben leaned out, ready to draw back the bolts.

"No need," said Leon, flushing a new green from where he crouched, hidden

202

on the flaking paint. He drew the bolt with his nimble fingers as if he had unlocked it many times before.

The hippo seemed unsurprised to find Leon there. "Any news?" was all he asked.

"The woman departed," said Leon. "But she saw more than is ideal. She might cause more trouble yet, so don't rush to the front of the building. She's guessed the boy is here and may wait outside, hoping to trap him when he leaves."

"But we've been in here ages," said Ben.

"Only a few minutes," said Leon.

"I guessed as much," said the hippo. "I think this mist can play with time, and placed us out of it for a little. But do not worry, Ben: this door is well hidden from the outside, and the path is overgrown. I don't think she will wait long in the cold for the sake of a mere suspicion. Humans are usually impatient and needlessly busy."

"There is still the risk from the river," said Leon. "Will you check that also?"

"I will," agreed the hippo. "Though I do not yet see what can be done about it."

Then the door swung open, and the hippo lumbered through to the outside as if this were not the first time he had done so.

The Weir

CHAPTER 27

The path behind the museum looked impassable to Ben, but the dead vegetation rustled and crackled and gave way when the hippo thrust through. Ben was slumped on the hippo's back, exhausted and silent. He felt as though his mind had crashed like an overloaded computer. He was aware of the scolding calls of the rooks and the scents of leaf mold and soaked earth, yet he didn't stir until they reached the river. There they halted. And Ben sat up, for the compelling rush of the weir refreshed him.

From the peninsula where the museum stood, the waterfall itself wasn't visible — they could see only the river plunging over the lip of the weir. The spume of white spray and the crash of the water signaled ferocious rapids beyond. In spite of all Mom's warnings, Ben felt excited. He longed to see more of it. The disused footbridge that ran above the weir was dilapidated and neglected — it didn't look safe — but the bulwarks of concrete supporting both ends appeared solid enough.

He had to raise his voice above the rumble of the weir. "D'you think the river's going to flood?"

"The weir is high," said the hippo. "Yet it has been this high before and never flooded. And whatever you have heard, Ben, I do not think that Julian Pike will be fool enough to climb up there and tamper with it. A fall from there would be deadly. The currents beneath the waterfall could hold a man under until he drowned."

"So — we shouldn't go closer," said Ben regretfully.

"It would be most unwise," said the hippo. The lines deepened on his face as he turned to look at Ben.

Ben avoided his stare by following the motion of one swift patch of river with his eyes. It hurtled past, gone in a swirling moment, yet instantly replenished by more. He dismounted. His sneakers sank into the waterlogged ground as he tried to imagine the amount of water that would flow through the weir in the next hour, and the next night, and the next day. When he thought of the power of it, he knew that there was nothing he could do if it should flood; the prospect of changing the course of these mighty currents was hopeless. It would be as futile as trying to change the flow of time.

Yet, for all that, he felt entranced by the power of the river. His worries seemed to float away, and he began to understand why his father had risked everything to go to sea.

The hippo seemed in no rush to return to the museum. He continued to walk companionably beside Ben, though he had positioned himself between the boy and the water as if to usher him away from the bank.

Ben guessed that the hippo didn't trust him to be sensible. "I'm sorry," he said. "Everything I did today went wrong. I know I shouldn't have opened the bottle."

"And you learned nothing?" said the hippo.

Ben took a last deep breath of waterfall air and thought of what he had discovered about himself. "I think I know who I am now. And I know a bit more about who my dad was."

"Isn't that what you came here to do?"

"Yes," Ben said, and then remembered something. "And I've got proof. The pufferfish said—"

"Do you need proof?"

"Well, my mom might." Ben patted the pocket that held the newspaper clipping, but was reminded of the silver bottle again, as he could feel it, cold and bulky, under his hand. "I could throw that bottle into the river," he said. "I could get rid of it."

"You could," said the hippo. "Yet it belongs to the museum."

"Do you want to take it back, then?"

"How?" said the hippo with a broad smile. "I am not blessed with hands or pockets. Return it yourself next time you visit."

Ben shivered. "How long do you really think that mist will stay in there?"

The hippo looked thoughtful. "I think it will linger for some time yet — you saw that it was evolving. But do remember, it can't change anything permanently. That is its nature. There are other forms of magic of a more lasting quality."

"I've been thinking about that," said Ben. "I think —" And he was going to mention an idea he had about the blue stone with the hole in it, but the hippo had begun to move more purposefully and now interrupted him: "You should be getting home. What would your mother say if she knew you were here?"

Ben grinned. "She'd say, 'I don't want to find out you've been hanging around near the weir.'"

"Well, then, you had better go quickly so no one does find

out. This is where I must leave you, as I ought to return to Constance now. She may need me. But if you follow the path along the side of the building, you will find a way to the road that avoids the front door."

"I left my bike in a bush near the beehive entrance," said Ben.

"Then it will be there still."

Ben moved away as quietly as he could — the dusk was spookily silent. And at last he reached the back of the rhododendron bush where his bike lay hidden. He was about to drag it out when he heard a cell phone ringing.

And he heard Tara Snow answer it.

Quick as a blink, Ben whisked under the bush. The woman was pacing horribly close by. Through the canopy he could see her pointed shoes approaching. He prayed that she was deep in the world of her phone and hadn't heard him. And he wondered, *Was she waiting there to catch me?*

She was speaking with anger. "You do realize I've been waiting here in the rain to speak with you?" Then she spat, "Yes, it *is* important. We've been turned down. The old woman knows everything."

Ben slunk backward. He was worried that she might look down and see his sneakers. He didn't think she had, not yet, though he was close enough to hear the angry roaring that issued from the phone.

It was Julian Pike's voice.

And there was a lot of swearing.

The rain pattered overhead, making Ben's hideout under the rubbery leaves feel like a tent. At any other time it might have felt almost cozy under there. Not today. Not with Tara Snow and her phone a few steps away.

"There was something very odd going on," she continued. "Some smoke that was almost as thick as mist. And I could have sworn I heard someone in the other room. I think it was the boy we saw yesterday. Who else could have told her about our plans?"

She paused while the man said something in a low voice. Ben's heart twanged in fear.

"Well, I did say I always suspected . . . I suppose she's not going to take what a kid tells her as gospel truth — no one's really going to believe him. All the same, you'd better do it soon, hadn't you? I'd like it over with."

Do what? Ben wondered.

He couldn't hear the man's words, but the menace in his voice was plain.

"Yes, in the next few days!" Tara Snow demanded. "Well, as soon as possible . . . There's supposed to be heavy rain tonight. . . . All right, how about tomorrow night, then?"

A car drove past the museum. By the time the sound of it faded, she was farther away from Ben's bush.

"I suppose I could have a look if you want," he heard her say. "I've got some boots in the car. You mean, go down there and check how high the water level is? If that's all, I guess I could —"

The remainder of what she said was swallowed by the clunk of a car door. Moments later an engine started and the car pulled away.

Her car?

Probably.

All the same, Ben waited until he was sure she had gone before he parted the leaves to look.

Water from the leaves trickled down his sleeves, but he saw nothing but twilight and rain. No one was around. Hastily he dragged his bike out and set off. Pedaling hard, he swept past the building site. Empty now: the builders had all gone home for the night, and the only sign of life was a beige car parked beside the gate with the light on its dashboard still fading as if someone had recently been inside. Ben had almost reached the bridge when it occurred to him that it could have been Tara Snow's car. if so, she had pulled up just a little bit farther on.

That was odd.

He wondered what Pike had told her to do.

He pulled over at the stopping place on the bridge and

peered toward the building site. He didn't really expect to see anything in the dark, but presently he spotted the pinprick glint of a flashlight. Then he saw the woman herself, her pale coat glowing softly in the reflected light from the river. She was standing near the bank beside two willow trees, which were all that remained of the grove that had once grown there. The trees leaned sharply over the water, black in the twilight, ugly and broken. They were very close to the edge. Soon, Ben supposed, they would be chopped down too. He wondered why they had been spared thus far. Maybe Tara Snow was wondering the same thing.

He stood watching her do nothing, until the hungry part of his brain began to clamor that if Mom had gone shopping after the meeting, he still might reach home before she did. Tara Snow had talked of doing something tomorrow night. Well, he would come back tomorrow in the day, and bring Mom, as Constance had asked, and then maybe everything would be all right. Maybe the sun would shine too and the mist would vanish as the witch had.

"And I'll bring Dad's stone," he murmured. "Just in case."

211

A History

Ben was back home before Mom. He supposed this was lucky, yet he felt very lonely as he clicked on the light. He found some ginger cookies and turned on the TV. That was better — he was home in time to catch a cartoon series he liked about a private detective who was a cat. The cat created havoc while it coolly solved the mystery and seemed to have no qualms about the chaos it had caused, and neither did anyone else. Ben wished it were the same in real life. *I wish I hadn't opened that bottle*, he thought as he munched.

He had eaten quite a lot of the cookies before he heard Mom's feet on the steps. He jumped up guiltily and switched the kettle on before rushing to the door to give her a hug.

"That's a nice welcome," she said, smiling through her obvious tiredness. "How was your day?"

"OK," he said. "How was the meeting?"

She took off her coat. The kettle boiled and he made the tea, then put the three cookies that were left on a plate so Mom wouldn't notice how many he had eaten.

"Ooh, is that a cup of tea?" she said with a sigh.

The weatherman came on the TV, warning of storms and concerns about local flooding.

"Not good," said Mom, pointing to the screen as she took the mug from him. "They were talking about that new building site by the river at the meeting. That developer was there to answer questions."

"The building site?" said Ben. "That's Julian Pike's."

"So I gather," she said dryly, "though goodness knows how you found that out."

"Did he say he's going to raise our rent?"

She frowned as she sipped her tea. She took one of the cookies, so he took one too. "Well, he didn't . . . but . . . Oh, he was so annoying. He wouldn't answer any of our questions properly and he clearly didn't want to be there. Actually, it was really rude — he kept looking at his phone while other people were talking. Then he told us he has a new project lined up just now and if it goes ahead they'll be busy with that for a couple of years. So, while I don't trust the man at all, I don't think much is going to happen here for some time."

"I bet the museum is his other project," said Ben.

Mom rolled her eyes. "Let's not go back to that now. Look, I've got to get a couple of e-mails off before supper. Can we talk about it later?"

"What's for supper?"

"Oh, Ben, do you mind eggs again? I bought some fresh bread this morning, and there's some jelly for you in the fridge."

"I don't feel like eggs," he said.

"Don't you?" Mom was surprised. "Well, I think there are some fish fingers, though you don't usually like them as much."

"I do now," said Ben.

But she was already halfway up the stairs.

He sighed and got out his homework. There was still one cookie left on the plate. He was thinking how lonely it looked when Mom shouted from the shop.

"Ben! Come here *right this minute.*" Her voice sounded peculiar.

He leaped up the stairs. "What?"

She was looking absolutely outraged! Then he saw that the computer screen was open on his forged letter.

"Oh ..."

"Is that all you have to say for yourself?"

"I'm sorry ... I had to ... I —"

"*I'm sorry?* There's *no excuse* for this, Ben. I've always trusted you. What *have* you been up to?"

"I had to go today. It was the only time the museum was open," he protested.

"You *had* to? No, Ben, you didn't *have* to do anything. That isn't a proper explanation. There's no excuse for forging letters to skip school."

He was shouting now too. "I *did* have to go. You wouldn't listen, so I had to find out more about Dad — and I *have!*"

After that outburst, he stormed off to his room. He sat on his bed, determined not to cry. Reaching in his pocket for a tissue, his fingers found the newspaper clipping....

Not long afterward, Mom knocked gently on his bedroom door. She came and sat next to him on the bed.

He handed her the piece of yellowed newsprint. She read it quietly.

"Where did you get this?"

"It was in the museum. On Miss Garner-Gee's mantelpiece."

"Did she give it to you?"

He ignored her question. "That's Dad, isn't it? And us. Why does it say we went away too?"

Mom gave a great sigh. "It was a mistake. Newspapers don't always get things right."

"But — you never told her it wasn't true. She thought..."

Mom breathed out impatiently. "Look, I never even met the

215

woman. And at the time I didn't want to. She was the one who encouraged your dad with his plans for one last voyage — after I'd begged him to give it all up."

"Was that when he took me to the museum?"

He thought she wasn't going to answer. She sighed heavily. But then she said, "Yes, he took you with him. It was the one time they ever met. She was some distant long-lost relative of his —"

"His granddad was her uncle."

"So you have talked to her," Mom said slowly. "Well, I suppose you must have if you've gotten that far."

"I didn't talk to her much about that," Ben said curtly. Then he shouted, "Why didn't you *tell* her we were still alive?"

"Because when your dad didn't come back, I blamed her!" Mom replied. She swept her hand over her eyes, and when she began speaking again, her voice was gentler. "I can see now that was very unfair. . . . But I was grieving, Ben. It was a hard time. Then, as the years went by, it seemed too late to go back and . . . Well, I thought she'd be dead, if I'm honest. When I heard they were building houses down there, I assumed the museum had gone."

"Didn't you check?"

"I suppose I should have. I didn't really want to think about it. There've been so many other things to worry about and . . . Ben, I don't think she even knew my name. I'd have felt — well — odd,

about just turning up there. I wasn't married to your dad, you know, so I didn't have any rights to anything. He was only some sort of second cousin to her. She might have thought I was . . . oh, I don't know . . . trying to get money out of her or something. Sometimes horrid people take advantage of old ladies."

"You said you met him in Australia."

"Yes." She nodded. Then she went silent, but he kept looking at her really hard, willing her to go on, and at last she began to talk again. "On the night your dad and I met we discovered that his family came from my hometown. Here — this town, I mean. I was feeling homesick at the time, so that seemed . . . sort of fateful. There we were on the other side of the world, yet weirdly connected. He told me how his great-grandfather's family had set up the museum. In my hometown! I wasn't much interested in museums in those days, so I'd never even seen it, but he talked about wanting to visit and, well, it kept us together for a while. That — but really very little else. I wanted a quiet life, you see. I wanted to come home, whereas he was an adventurer. Really, Ben, it's a hard life to be the partner of an explorer.

"In the end I decided I couldn't bear it. I left him and I came back here. That's when I found out I was going to have a baby — you! So this is the town where you were born. And your dad didn't even know about you — not then, anyway. But

217

when you were about two years old, he turned up. He'd come from the other side of the world to find me. He was amazed and delighted to find you too.

"He loved you so much, Ben, and for a while we were all really happy. He promised to give up his sea adventures and settle down with us. He said he was going to look up his relative — apparently she had offered him work. But after he went to that museum, it all began again.

"He wanted to go on one last voyage. I tried to persuade him not to — for your sake as well as mine. But . . ." She sighed and her voice trailed off. "Well, you know the rest."

"Maybe Garner-Gees have to explore," mumbled Ben. "I'm one too. That's how I found the museum."

"I'm realizing that," she said grimly.

"The museum's amazing," he blurted out. "But Mom, it's in trouble. That man — that Pike man — he really does want to buy it and knock it down, and if Miss Garner-Gee doesn't agree to sell it to him, he's going to flood it, so that then she'll have no choice."

"Ben, that sounds a bit over the top. Wherever did you get that idea?"

He explained what he had heard in the café.

"And you told the old lady?"

"Yes. But . . . I don't know if she believed me about the flood."

"Does she know who you are?"

Ben hesitated. "I think she's worked it out. And Mom, she's a very old lady now, and there aren't any *other* relatives. Just me."

She took a deep breath. "Well, I suppose I'd better come with you next time."

"Can we go now?"

"Don't be silly."

"But —"

"No, Ben. No one's going out there tonight. Look at that rain: it's bucketing down." She took his hand and unwrapped his fingers. Then she put Dad's stone into his palm. "You left this next to the computer."

He blinked down at it. "Is that how you knew about the note?"

"It made me suspicious, certainly. Come on. Let's go and put those eggs on to boil. I've bought some lovely crusty bread."

Ben guessed she had forgotten about the fish fingers. "All right, then, eggs," he said. "But afterward, *I'm* going to tell you a different magic story. One about a witch in a bottle, and a hippo ..."

"I'm not sure I can take magic on top of all this," Mom said with a laugh.

"You're going to have to," he said, holding out his arms. "This time it's true."

Stormy Weather

CHAPTER 29

Later that night the lightning crackled and rain pounded the pavement, and it was weather for huddling — not for flying. Yet a few bees were out in the storm, riding the wind until they reached a rooftop far away from their hive.

They swooped into the chimney. It was black down there, but the soot from a disused fire was sparse and ancient, so they were safe enough. Down they dived until at the very bottom they found a crack of paler dark. Then, one by one, they wriggled through to the human side of a boarded-up fireplace. In the room, they regrouped, leaving sooty smears on the wallpaper as they dried their sodden wings....

Ben was suddenly wide awake. Had the thunder woken him? The image of his broken dream was still vivid — he could almost see it in front of him. He had dreamed of the riverbank, with those two ragged trees blasted by lightning against the night.

He sat bolt upright. "Mom!"

She must have been lying awake too, because she was with

him in an instant. "You all right? Did the thunder frighten you?"

"I'm not a baby," he protested.

"No. No, but it's quite a storm. Listen to that rain."

"Mom, I've thought of something. What would happen if a big tree fell into the weir?"

"Ben, do we have to talk about this in the middle of the night?"

"Yes, we do. What would happen if a tree got stuck in the weir?"

"Well, I expect it could . . . flood. . . ." Her voice trailed away on the last word.

"That's it, isn't it? That's how they'll flood the museum."

"Are there trees near the bank?"

"There's two left on the building site, right at the edge of the water. I noticed them —" He gulped, suddenly fearful that his mom would know he had been near the water. He added hastily, "From a safe place, Mom — I saw it from up on the bridge, and it was obvious because all the others have been chopped down. They looked all wrong. What if he kept them just so he could push them in at the right moment?"

Mom was silent, but from her expression, he knew she thought it was possible.

Ben swung out of bed. "By the time anyone sees what's happened, it'll be too late, won't it? The museum will have flooded."

"Ben"—she was shaking her head—"no one will be going out there tonight."

"I bet he is, and I am too!"

"No, you're NOT! Ben, I do *not* want you near any river in the middle of a storm like this. Is that clear? If I thought there was any reason to do something tonight, I'd call the police." She gave him a hug. "I'll go with you in the morning. But for now, please, *go back to sleep.*"

Ben put Dad's stone around his neck before he lay down again. But he couldn't sleep. He tried counting sheep. He tried counting hippos. He turned over and opened his eyes.

"Mom!"

She came rushing back. "What now?"

"Look!" He pointed at the boarded-up fireplace. There was a crack along one side of it. Through the crack wriggled a bee, then another, and another, and they joined more already clustering on the wall.

"What on earth?" gasped Mom. "Oh, the storm must have disturbed their nest. Come out of here, Ben. I'll call pest control in the morning."

"No! Wait. They've come to find us!" said Ben. "Look."

The bees had formed themselves into a wobbly word:

NOW

"Now do you believe me?"

Mom stared. Then she bumped down on his bed. "Don't know if I can believe my eyes right now."

"I told you. They know things. So do some of the other animals."

"Ben, you can't expect me to believe . . ." She trailed off as she watched the bees re-form themselves. This time they made two words:

OR NEVER

At last she stood up. "All right, I'll call the police." She looked shaky but determined as she marched to the phone.

Ben followed anxiously.

So did the bees.

However, Mom seemed to be convinced now. Ben watched her explain the situation over the phone. He lolled against her; it was good to be believed. "Yes," she said into the phone, then a little less calmly, "*Yes, tonight!*" Then she began to frown. "Well, I have reason to be suspicious. There's potential for flooding near the weir and"— she began to sound exasperated —"yes, I know there's a storm, but doesn't that mean . . ."

Ben fiddled with the shoelace around his neck. This was all taking too long. On the phone Mom raised her voice a little: "Well, yes, the man in question *does* own the property, but I still think you should go right away because . . . Well, when *can* you get there?"

There was a long silence while someone talked back, but Ben couldn't hear it. He was so impatient that his bones felt itchy. Couldn't he and Mom go and check the river themselves? He rolled Dad's stone in his hand. He wished his dad were with them. *Dad was brave*, thought Ben. *He'd have gone out there like a shot.* Immediately he felt guilty for such a disloyal thought. After all, he and Mom had managed very well until now. He hugged her tight around the waist to make up for the mean thought.

"Yes . . . I can see that." It sounded like Mom was finishing up. "Yes, I understand. Well, thanks very much." She bumped the phone down rather hard. "There's some power cables down, so they're very busy," she said with a sigh. "They're going to send a patrol car later."

"But . . . how will they know where to go?" said Ben. "You

didn't give them an address. You didn't say which part of the river."

Mom was suddenly furious. "D'y'know what? They didn't ask for an address, did they? I don't think they believed a word I was saying. They think I'm just a silly woman who's had a bad dream. I bet they won't send anyone at all."

"Don't they have to, now that you've reported it?"

"Well . . . possibly . . . Oh, I expect they'll send a car over to look at the weir *sometime* before morning — but they didn't say *when.*"

"What're we going to do?"

Mom looked at the floor, lips clamped together. Then she nodded sharply. "Get dressed. We'll go ourselves."

"Really?" exclaimed Ben.

Ten minutes later, when they unlocked the front door, the bees swooped out before them and disappeared into the blustering dark.

Ben was dismayed.

"I expect they know what they're doing," Mom reassured him as they mounted their bikes. "Maybe this storm will blow them back double-fast."

What if it doesn't? worried Ben.

Yet there was no chance to talk as they rode: rain battered

their faces and the wind buffeted their bikes, and flooding gutters spewed across the tarmac, making the going treacherous. When they reached the bridge, the crosswinds were so intense that they dared spare only an occasional glance over the parapet. But that was enough to see that the river looked dangerously wide, wider than it ever should have been: a seething brew, churning with reflections from the streetlights and the inky black shadows.

Before they turned onto Dial Avenue, Mom pulled over. She switched off her bike lights and indicated that Ben should do the same.

"But that's dangerous!" Ben protested.

Mom chuckled. "Bit late to be worrying about danger, now that you've dragged us out to catch a dastardly builder in the middle of the night. Better if we're not seen, don't you think?"

Ben swallowed. "So you think he might be down there?"

"I'd like to catch him at it if he is. Then we can report him."

"I wish we had a cell phone."

"Well, we don't," she said. "You know mine's broken. There's no way I can afford to replace it right now. Come on, we'll be very careful not to be seen by anyone."

By night Dial Avenue was a secret, silent place, as the glitter of the river didn't reach the road and there were fewer streetlights. Before long, the row of houses on one side of the road was replaced by the fence that hid the building site. Nailed amid the stained posters advertising long-gone rock bands was a new notice board with drawings of the proposed houses and a sign that proclaimed:

"Those'll sell for a fortune," growled Mom.

But Ben said nothing at all. Instead he pointed at the building-site gate, which was swinging in the wind.

Mom braked.

So did Ben.

He caught her eye, and in silence they pulled their bikes over and leaned them against the fence. The peril seemed more real now: Ben could almost taste it, sour as curdled milk.

"I suppose someone could have left it open," whispered Mom. "Are we just going to walk in?"

Mom peered through the gates, and the light of battle gleamed in her eyes. "I don't see why not," she replied. "I need to see if those trees are still there."

Trespassing

CHAPTER 30

From the building site, they could see the museum set back among trees. It stood on its wooded peninsula, which entirely blocked any view of the weir.

"I can see why Pike wants to get his hands on that land," murmured Mom. "Right next door, isn't it? If he takes down that museum, he'll be able to build three times as many houses and make even more money."

"We're not going to let him," said Ben.

In spite of the cold, he unzipped his coat at the top and clutched Dad's stone for luck as they passed among dark unfinished houses and cement mixers and heaps of bricks and rubble and gravel, where hulking diggers hunched in the dark like war machines. Drainage pipes were stacked like missiles, canvas flapped, and everywhere was mud and more mud in deep trenches and puddles.

The storm rumbled on. As Ben faced the riverbank, the growling clouds flashed. And he saw, in that bright lightning moment, that only one of those riverbank trees was stamped

against the white sky. The other tree was gone! And there was a digger lurking right where it had stood.

"What's the matter?" said Mom.

"One of the trees by the river is down!" he gasped.

"Are you sure?"

"I think so."

They both peered into the blackness. It was too dark to be certain.

"I think there was a digger down there too."

She looked sharply at him, and then at the ground, biting her lip. "I think you're right," she said. "Look over there. Those are digger tracks and they're fresh. See? There's no water in them yet. Someone drove one toward the riverbank very recently."

"So — he's down there, isn't he?"

They both stood in silence, searching the dark.

"Maybe not," Mom said, "but I bet the evidence'll be gone by the morning if this water keeps rising."

"Come on, then," said Ben, grabbing his mom and pulling her toward the river.

"No, Ben. Hang on." She pulled him back. "This is getting really dangerous. If he's there, he's in a digger. I didn't expect that. This isn't something I want you mixed up in. He might ..." Her voice trailed away anxiously. Then she said, "I think it's time we got help. Let's find a phone and call the police again — we've seen enough now to call them out."

"And give him time to push the other tree in?" Ben was incredulous: he couldn't believe Mom could back out. Yet her shoulders were hunched and her body twisted toward the gate. He knew she was about to insist that they leave. He couldn't bear it. In desperation he said something really cruel: "Dad wouldn't have given up so easily."

He regretted that instantly. Her face crumpled as if she had been slapped. Now he couldn't bear to look at her, couldn't bear that he'd hurt her, couldn't bear that she'd forced him to say such a horrible thing.

"Well, I'm going anyway," he cried as he pulled away. He fled along the tracks the digger had made.

"Wait!" she called after him. "All right, I'm coming."

Ben didn't wait; he kept on running until the worn soles of his boots lost their grip on the slippery clay and he skidded out of control.

He fell flat on the ground.

She caught up. She smiled down at him sadly, then hauled him onto his feet. He was coated in mud — even on his face. "Now you're really in disguise" was all she said.

He couldn't look her in the eyes.

It didn't matter. She hugged him in spite of the mud, although that made her filthy too. And still holding on to him she turned them both toward a long ridge of banked earth that had been thrown up by the diggers. It ran most of the length of the riverbank.

"See that, Ben?" She pointed. "I figure that huge mound of earth's been dumped there on purpose to stop the building site from flooding. It'll channel any flood toward the museum. But if we climb up there, we should be able to see exactly what's going on. When we do, we'll make a decision."

He nodded.

She turned and led the way at a sensible pace. He followed, still feeling ashamed, but there wasn't much time for dwelling on the awful thing he had said because he had to scramble up that bank of sodden crumbling clay. And that was tricky. Both of them slipped onto their hands more than once and their legs grew heavy with mud. Nevertheless, when they reached the top of the ridge, it was worth it.

They could see everything. The river, a foaming torrent beneath, was washing around the base of a lone willow tree. The other tree was gone. But there, out across the water, in the very center of the weir, they could make out its dark, knotted shape. It was already acting like a dam, preventing the turbulent currents from flowing freely downriver. And the water was rising fast.

"Gosh, he planned this carefully," said Mom. "That tree

landed exactly where it would cause the most blockage. He must know these currents very well. I bet the river'll cover his tracks too." She indicated the remaining tree and the churned-up earth around it. Telltale tracks pointed from the place where the other tree had stood, toward a digger, which was parked a little way off. The cab of the digger was dark. It looked empty. "Come on, Ben. Seems like he's gone, but at least we can report what we've seen."

Even as she turned, a sudden light blasted from the base of the mound and a voice snarled, "It's me who should be doing the reporting. What the hell are you doing on my land at two o'clock in the morning?"

They were dazzled. Behind the light, they could see the bulky shadow of the man holding the flashlight: a narrow oblong head, hulking shoulders, heavy boots. Julian Pike!

Ben was terrified. He tugged at Mom. "Let's go."

Yet Mom was as fierce as a mother goose confronting a bull. "Mr. Pike, there's a tree from your land blocking the weir. It's about to flood the museum property. What are you going to do about it?"

"Excuse me?" The man barked a laugh — an ugly little sound. "I've driven down here to stop the other one from falling in. Why are *you* here?"

Mom pushed Ben behind her and pointed to the digger.

"Don't give me that nonsense. You helped that tree into the water, didn't you?"

"Are you *accusing* me of something? Yer mad, woman!"

Ben felt the blood drain from his face and the skin around his mouth grow rigid. He tugged Mom again. "Let's go."

She ignored him. Fearlessly she moved to shield Ben, and fixing Pike with her most powerful scowl, she said, "I'm suggesting you had something to do with it."

The flashlight underlit the man's face. He looked demon-like. "You got some nerve!" he roared.

Abruptly he bounded up the slope.

Ben shrank in horror.

Mom stood her ground.

But as the man's heavy boots struck the summit, his sheer weight sent a tremor through the soaked earth. The clay atop the mound began to crack and shudder. Then it slid. Mom, by now nearest the edge, lurched backward on a chunk of shifting mud. Her feet slipped. Her elbows flailed. She flung up an arm but grasped only sky.

"Mom!" Ben screamed.

"Hey!" yelled Pike. "Steady there, Mrs. —"

Mom screamed, and then it was as if the sky swung sideways, and the river reached for her while the earth shrugged, pitching her into the waiting water —

SPLASH!

There was a split-white second when time reared up like the cascade of spray, and the moment froze. Then the current swept Mom away, and the urgent present burst back, clear as a bubble.

Hunted

"YOU CAN'T HAVE MY MOM!" The anguished scream came twisting from Ben, tearing at his throat, his soul, his heart, as the river thundered by, foaming and hissing, wild and ancient, carrying Mom away as it had doubtless carried so many before. He leaped to the water's edge, distraught, desperate, but with no idea how to save her.

Pike dragged him back. "Don't be a fool. You jump in after her and I'll have two of you to haul out!"

He gripped Ben by the shoulders as they watched Mom flounder in the surging flood, saw her fight, saw her lose the first battle as the water dragged her under its black weight.

"Is she a strong swimmer?" the man barked.

"Yes," cried Ben, wriggling free. "Yes, she's really good." And he shouted to Mom, promising they'd save her, begging her not to give up. His voice didn't carry over the river's rush, but he saw her bob to the surface again, lashing and thrashing, head held high until the careless current swept her out to the center of the river.

There, they lost sight of her.

Ben turned to Julian Pike, pleading in anguish, "We've got to rescue her."

Pike sucked his teeth. "She might make it." He pulled out his flashlight and sidled nearer to the edge, shining its beam across the heaving torrent. "I can't swim in that," he grunted. "We'll need rope." His teeth flashed in the light, and once again Ben noticed that he seemed to have more teeth than most people.

"Can't you phone the police?" he begged.

"No reception down here," said the man smoothly. "We'll have to go nearer the road."

Ben ached for a grown-up, organized rescue. He was desperate to trust someone, anyone, even Pike, whom he didn't trust at all. He searched the man's face, yearning to find kindness, or at least some sign of decency. Instead he glimpsed a slurring in those piggy eyes and the tiniest twitch that somehow warned him of immediate danger.

Julian Pike lunged.

But Ben ducked. He escaped the grasping hands and fled.

Pike bellowed and launched himself after Ben — but his heavy weight hampered his progress on the mud.

Ben may have had short legs, but he was light and nimble, and terror lent him unexpected speed. As he sprang up the mound, he felt absolutely certain that Julian Pike wanted to push him into the river after Mom. First, though, he'd have to catch him.

The man almost did: Ben felt a hand snatching at his coat, but by then he'd reached the top of the mound; he wrenched free and hurled himself downhill into the dark.

At the bottom of the ridge, there was no reflected light from the river. Ben plunged full tilt into blackness, switching direction, swerving sideways rather than sprinting straight for the road, because he hoped that way he might lose Pike, and then he'd double back to the riverbank and find a way to rescue Mom.

Click! The man's flashlight turned on.

The ground became a black and silver turmoil as Ben's flying shadow dodged and wove. So, now the man knew where he was. Yet the light helped Ben negotiate the worst of the ditches so that his speed actually increased. Pike must have realized this, because the light blinked off again, throwing them into fresh darkness while Ben ran like a rabbit, ran like the weather, splashing and sliding through trenches, slipping often but somehow always stumble-lunging upright, until he felt almost outside himself, as if he were watching something that was happening to someone else. He ran among the half-built houses, a labyrinth of brick walls that were well known to Julian Pike whereas Ben knew them not at all. So that was a mistake.

The distance between them closed. The pounding of the builder's boots and the heavy grunts of his breathing grew louder. Every so often the flashlight's beam caught Ben or his shifting shadow, and each time, it seemed nearer and brighter. And he was tiring now. A stitch began to knot in his side as he bolted down a passage between two newly built walls. The pain mounted, sharp as a shark's tooth. He needed to pause until it eased. He turned a  corner and darted into a half-completed building with no roof and doubled up against a wall, massaging his side, panting as quietly as he could, waiting, hoping.

The man lumbered past.

Had he lost him?

Ben thought he had.

Wrong! Suddenly, horribly, the flashlight shone into his hiding place, catching him huddled by the half-finished wall, with no other exit.

The man began to advance, panting heavy, jagged breaths.

Terror drove Ben over the wall. He scrambled like a cat, hardly feeling skinned shins, torn nails, or the jarring of his knees when he landed on the other side. Pike gave a bellow of rage, but Ben was already swerving from that churned-up passage, heart walloping his ribs to the beat of his feet as he raced away from the buildings.

He was close to exhaustion now. Yet Pike was catching up to him. And something else was catching up too: that stark image of Mom's fall into the river flooded Ben's mind, stopped his throat, filled his eyes with tears so that he couldn't see, and then, all at once, here was another ditch. The glint of water at the bottom saved him from falling straight in. He leaped at the last minute, narrowly missing it, then landed awkwardly and staggered one more wobbly step. Then he was down, curled in the mud, trembling. And Julian Pike was almost upon him.

He would be caught.

Then what?

His hand clutched for Dad's stone and he squeezed it, pleading silently, begging the night to make him invisible.

A few feet away, Pike halted, cursing. The flashlight clicked on. It scanned the ground from side to side.

Yet by some miracle, the light didn't fall where Ben lay. It missed him. Pike eventually ran on, leaving him crouching in the mud, caught instead by the unbearable knowledge that all this was his fault.

The Roughest Day

CHAPTER 32

Ben rolled sideways. His chest hurt and the stitch in his side twisted. But that wasn't the worst of it. Agonizing thoughts of Mom in the water tortured him now, crippled him. Could he bear to return to the river? Could he stare into that empty dark, fearing that Mom wouldn't come back? There: he'd let the worst fear-thought loose — *maybe she'd drowned*. But the idea was unendurable. He clutched at his head, screwing his eyes tighter to push the dread away. That didn't work, because it was inside him, and he was overwhelmed with the urge to curl up and hide like a wounded animal.

There was a hiding place too; ahead of him stood a stack of drainage pipes. Hardly able to think, Ben chose a pipe on the bottom row. Only a child could have crawled into that narrow hole — which made it all the more suitable.

Inside the pipe, it was pitch-dark. It smelled of dead things, and there was a puddle of stagnant water in the base of it. But Ben was too exhausted to care about anything except the knowledge that Pike wouldn't be able to follow him inside.

Furthermore, there were two exits — two escape routes — one at each end. He crawled until he reached the middle, and there, with cheek and shoulder pressing against slimy concrete, he sat in that cold puddle nursing his unbearable misery. Fear coiled around him like a giant snake, squeezing him almost senseless. And though he knew that the longer he waited, the smaller his chance would be of ever saving Mom, he felt quite unable to do anything but clutch at the blue stone. He gripped it until the edges dug sharply into his hand, and he focused on the numb, real hurt of that, welcoming the small pain because he thought he deserved it.

He prayed, whispered, repeated in despair: "Please help me! Please help my mom!"

A little while later, he heard a soft thud overhead. He opened his eyes. There was definitely a faint shuffling sound. Then, somewhere near the front of the pipe, he heard a gentle splash.

Ben cowered. Could it be Pike sneaking back? No, he thought, calming himself; the scuffling, whatever it might be, was too quiet to be human. Just night noises, then? He could hear rain plinking on the pipes. He could hear the river, hear the wind scraping through the trees — nothing more. Yet he still felt uneasy. He decided he was ready to move after all.

He had begun to shift toward the entrance when he heard Pike returning. There was no doubting the real thing; the man was too hefty to move quietly. His heavy boots squelched. His clothes flapped; his breathing was angry, smoker's hoarse. Ben froze. Now the man was moving along the pipes. Did he suspect something? Was he checking each one?

The flashlight's beam swung into Ben's pipe. It dazzled. The arc of light flicked over the walls, and Ben glimpsed green slime and soaked concrete. The light crept closer to his toes . . .

SPLASH!

Something stirred near the entrance. The man gave a shout of surprise and the flashlight turned toward the sound.

"A stinkin' rat!" cursed Pike, leaping back.

Ben glimpsed the head and ears of a rodent near the entrance to the pipe. Then the man left Ben in the dark — with the rat. He sat tensely, knowing he shouldn't cry out, even if it jumped at him.

Would it bite?

Outside, framed by the round entrance to the pipe, he could see the progress of the light. It looked as if the man was searching elsewhere. Ben tried to concentrate on that rather than on the rat, though he couldn't help imagining the rat sneaking closer. He cringed, half expecting to feel its squirming touch, then began to shunt himself gently toward the back exit — it was darker at that end and closer to the river.

That was when the rat leaped.

Ben didn't scream. He cowered, with his hands protecting his face, flinching — whereupon the rat hopped into his top pocket and began to scold: "Holy slime mold! What do you think you're doing here at this hour — enjoying a bit of night air?"

Obviously, it wasn't a rat at all — it was the sengi. And what's more, the shadow shape of Flummery's head peered over the edge of the back exit. He was perching in the pipe above Ben's head.

"Well, bless my feathers," the owl hooted. "The bees were right! He *is* nesting in one of these stone tubes."

"I am *not* nesting," growled Ben, though hope flowed through him like hot soup as he crawled toward Flummery. He had never been so glad to be scolded and teased in all of his life — which was fortunate, because there was more to come.

"Did your nap do you good?" said the sengi. "Are you ready

to see your poor mother? I expect she's worried about you."

"Worried about me?" Ben's voice came out hoarse and desperate.

"Of course she's worrying about you," said the owl. "Doesn't she always?"

"You sound like you know where she is," he said as he scrambled from the pipe, his voice rough with relief. "Is she all right?"

"Well, the bees say she's safer than she was," said Flummery. "Best follow me," he urged. And before Ben had a chance to ask more questions, the owl launched into the air. After that, Ben could see only a dark owl-shape against the heavy sky, beckoning.

Feeling almost dizzy with relief, he hastened to follow. All the same, he thought the owl had sounded evasive, as if there were something he wasn't telling him. As for the sengi, all she would say was "Wait and see," though she was gnawing at her tail again, and Ben knew by now that this was a sign she was worried.

248

To his surprise, Flummery didn't head to the right of the mound where Mom had fallen. Instead he flew to the far left, where the heaped earth sloped gently toward the museum. Hidden beyond it was a short spit of land that stretched into the river. This had once been cordoned off, though all that remained of that broken fence was a few wooden stakes, and Flummery landed on one of these. When Ben caught up, he saw that the owl was staring across the water at a small round sea vessel. It was far away, but as it sailed toward them, it glowed like a fallen moon.

A Strange River Craft

CHAPTER 33

The boat twirled as it rode the storm, and the waves carried it up and down. Ben thought it resembled the fairground ride with the spinning teacups. Gradually it whirled nearer, and to his amazement, he saw that the sailors on board were the witch and her green metallic beetle.

Their boat had to be the elephant bird's egg, although by some strange magic everything looked larger than it had been before. The witch seemed about the size of a slender child as she handled the tiller. The beetle, now about the size of a cat, was perched on the boom, hauling on ropes that shone like spiders' silk, until the sail swung away to one side. And the next time the boat turned about, Ben spotted a passenger.

Mom.

Immediately the sengi said, "Don't attract her attention. She might jump up and capsize the boat."

Ben longed to shout to her, but he saw that the sengi could be right. He could tell Mom was trying to look calm, but she wasn't quite succeeding as she sat there in the base of the shell with her tense white face peering over the jagged edge.

"I bet the witch rescued her because of all those eggshells she's saved," said Ben in an agony of nerves. "I used to think she told that story because she wasn't brave enough to talk about the truth. But she's being braver than me tonight."

"Perhaps your mom was always being brave," said Flummery softly. "People often are, even when you don't notice."

Somewhere out in the darkness, the digger coughed into life. The sound was distant. But it meant that Pike was still around.

The sengi scrambled from Ben's pocket and stood on her haunches, craning to hear. "Oh, I wish they'd hurry up and land," she cried.

Meanwhile, the boat was tacking to and fro, but stormy gusts kept blowing it off the shore. Sometimes the witch drew close enough for Ben to see the glint of her metal teeth. She was grinning as though she was enjoying this struggle with the weather. He still wasn't sure he trusted her, though, and out of habit he clutched at the shoelace. This time, as the cool edge of stone bit into his hand, he had an idea. Feeling urgent and excited, he tugged the lace over his head.

"Flummery, I need you to do something for me," he said. He held the stone up so they could see its glint. "This was my dad's. I've had it for ages. I just didn't know what it was. I think it belongs in the museum. Will you take it to Constance? It might be important."

There was a bloom of hope in the owl's eye as he replied, "No. You should take it to Constance."

"But there might not be time," Ben began to plead. "At least promise you'll take it if"—he swallowed—"if something bad happens?"

"You don't know for sure what it is," fussed the sengi. She was running back and forth across Ben's shoulder by now. "Anyway," she said, "Constance certainly wouldn't approve of us leaving you alone."

Ben gave the owl a long, level look. "I think it would be safer with you," he insisted. "If there's any trouble, you could fly."

A gust of wind brought another snatch of sound from the digger. It sounded closer. Flummery swiveled his head toward the engine noise, and when he turned back to Ben, there was deep concern in his eyes. He didn't object when Ben looped the shoelace over his neck and arranged the stone so it was hidden among his feathers.

"Well, for goodness' sake, don't go anywhere yet," squeaked the sengi. "They're bound to land soon."

"Not with this current," fretted the owl. "It keeps dragging them back."

The beetle seemed to think so too. As they watched, it grew visibly impatient. So did the witch. All of a sudden she threw both hands into the air. Immediately the tiller spun like a windmill, the boat pitched, and the mast collapsed; it bent like a sodden drinking straw until the sail crumpled, fabric rupturing like a broken petal.

Ben darted forward. He was terrified they would capsize. Yet the eggshell boat bobbed upright, and free of its sail it actually rode higher and more smoothly in the water. Directly after that, the witch and the beetle produced large spoon-shaped paddles and rowed the shell through the wind and the waves. At last they bumped against the bank. Even then, the egg looked poised to drift back into the current, but its spinning increased, faster and faster, until with a mighty heave it gyrated right out of the water, twisting up and along the bank in an elaborate roll before beaching on its side.

Mom tipped out onto the grass, safe. And Ben was right there, pulling her up, and then she was sweeping him into one of her tightest hugs, and for a few precious moments the world felt as if only they were in it.

The sengi's fussing put a stop to that. "Are you trying to squish me?" she complained.

Mom jumped.

"I told you about them," Ben said.

"Different to see it, though," Mom whispered. She eyed the sengi with a short puff of breath that was meant to be a laugh but wasn't quite.

The beetle remained in the eggshell. The witch had already

climbed out. She was tending to the shell, smoothing it with her hands. "Most grown-folks believe only what they understand," she said with a chuckle as she groomed the shell. "It makes them feel safer."

"Oh, I'm not going to pretend to understand," said Mom. "But I'm terribly grateful."

"And so am I," said Ben. "I knew you weren't bad."

The witch shrugged. "I once had hopes of being truly wicked," she said. "A conscience is a burden for a witch."

"Please!" said the sengi, fidgeting with nerves. "Can't we hurry? That man's still about, you know."

"Mr. Pike?" said Mom, looking blank. She still hadn't fully grasped the danger. "Where did he get to? I bet he didn't call any rescue out for me."

"It's worse than that," said Ben.

Only then did Mom notice the digger sounds. Her eyes grew wide, and she began to tug at Ben, pulling him away.

"Stay where you are—unless you want to run into him," warned the witch.

"Couldn't you take them both away by boat?" Flummery begged.

"No, it can't carry the two of them. And there's no time to conjure clever magic, so you'll have to use something else instead."

"Like what?"

The witch turned to Ben with narrowed eyes. "Do you still have that bottle?

Ben nodded, patting his pocket.

"Mind . . . point it at me again and you'll never be so sorry."

"I wouldn't."

"Then listen," said the witch. "We'll double up what magic we have. I can't shrink you small with an eggshell spell — that'll only work for us — but the bottle magic ought to be extra-strong if both spells are cast simultaneously."

"How?" said Ben.

But before the witch could answer, Mom grabbed him, tugging him away, because the roof of the digger had crested the far end of the mound. Yet where could they run to? They were on that long finger of land with the river racing on three sides of them, and the digger was about to block their route to drier ground.

Julian Pike Is Brought Down to Size

CHAPTER 34

Reflections of light from the river rippled across the digger. They flickered into the cab, and when they shone on Julian Pike no one doubted his intentions, as his face was twisted into a savage leer. They guessed he intended to crush them or push them into the flood — if he could.

Now the engine idled.

Slowly the massive back wheels began to swivel. Then the headlights snapped on, casting all but the silver streaks of diagonal rain into a black confusion.

Was there another escape route?

Ben searched for one with no success, though he thought for a moment that he glimpsed a bulk of darker blackness crossing behind the machine. However, he couldn't be sure what it was, or whether he'd even seen it at all, because the headlights were angling toward them now, and soon they blazed like murderous maniac-eyes directly into his face. Then the engine roared its challenge, poisoning the night with a belch of exhaust before it powered straight at them.

Dazzled and bewildered, they recoiled — all except Flummery, who took to the air.

"He's taking the stone to Constance," Ben cried.

"No, he's not!" screeched the sengi. "Oh, the fool: he thinks he can fight a digger!"

This seemed horribly true. Flummery, having gained height, dropped like a blade and challenged the hulking great engine like a parent bird protecting a nest. He squawked and pecked at the windshield. He pummeled the glass with his wings. He blocked the driver's forward view.

The machine fought back. The scooping arm raked the air as it aimed to smash the owl. Flummery reacted by hugging the glass where the digger arm couldn't quite reach him. He tore into the windshield wipers with his talons, and when Pike's hand came stretching from the side window, the owl swiped and clawed into the groping flesh. Then, when Pike's bleeding hand withdrew, Flummery pursued, squeezing through the window of the cab. There was a yelp of pain as Flummery attacked. The cab light flickered on, revealing a tumult of feathers and fists. The engine spluttered. The cab rocked and clanked until it seemed likely to tip over on the uneven ground.

Mom grabbed Ben. "Come on! Your owl's giving us a chance to get away."

"Too risky!" cried the witch, blocking their path. "He'll push you back with the fishes if you try to get past. Think again. *Use the bottle.*"

"You told me I needed magic words," said Ben, though he pulled it from his pocket.

"There's a lot said about magic words," said the witch with a grin. "But they're only instructions. The important part is to say what you mean with your whole heart."

"I'll try," said Ben, "but what words shall I say?"

The witch rolled her eyes. "You need to say *Take prisoners.* Those were the words I heard before that bottle trapped me for a hundred years."

"That's all?"

"It worked well enough to keep me stuck in there," she said, scowling, "though one more thing: if this shell spell's to be potent, I'll need your mother to spin."

"Spin?" Mom sounded panicky. "Oh, I'll do anything, but I don't understand what you want me to do."

"Widdershins," said the witch.

Mom looked desperate.

"She means spin counterclockwise," squeaked the sengi.

Ben was intent and urgent. "Don't you remember your story, Mom? The girl had to spin on her heels at the end." He would have added more to make sure she understood, but just then something hideous happened.

Inside the cab, a flailing fist dealt Flummery a mighty *thwack*, and the owl ricocheted through the window. He slammed to earth with a sickly thump, tumbling into the black.

This time it was Mom who dragged Ben back. She held him tight as Pike leaned from his window, grinning like a shark while his engine revved into reverse. Then the monster wheels began to roll: backward, forward, sideways, backward, forward, sideways — again and again, again and again, until it seemed certain that anything on the ground nearby would be crushed.

"Ready to use that bottle?" said the witch.

"Yes!" howled Ben. He twisted away from Mom and leaped into the path where the machine was headed.

Behind him, he dimly heard Mom protest.

"Stand firm," screeched the sengi. "Ben, this is your only chance."

The machine roared into a gully. There was a stench of diesel as it reappeared, headlights angled at the sky while it climbed the last slope. Once it reached the summit, the lights would plunge again, and it would be upon them.

The sengi scrambled to Ben's shoulder, yapping instructions. In the headlights her eyes shone like silver pins. Ben did as she bid, hunkering down on one knee like a hunter awaiting a wild beast. He wished he had a magic spear — an incredibly long one, which the digger would run onto like a wild boar. Instead he had this small silver bottle that he didn't fully trust. All the same, he forced himself to believe in it with all his heart as he pulled out the stopper and, pointing the end at his quarry, shouted: "*Take prisoners!*"

Nothing much happened at first. Ben had time to imagine how Captain Garner-Gee must have felt as he hunted large animals in Africa, and he had time to wonder if he, Ben Makepeace, his great-great-grandchild, was being tested, or punished for all the hunting his ancestors had done, and he almost had time to panic. Then, without warning, the bottle jolted and felt as hot as a freshly boiled egg — so hot, in fact, that he almost dropped it as a wavy brilliant shot of power burst out across his fingers. After that, the bottle felt cool again.

"Steady, steady . . ." said the sengi, as their view was blocked by a vast sheet of muddy water.

When the digger belted through, they saw that something astonishing had happened. It had shrunk. It was now the size of a small car!

"Excellent," said the sengi. "Now do it all over again." Ben wished he had a moment to turn and check on Mom. But he had no time; the sengi was squeaking like a cheap violin: "Idiot boy, we'll be in the drink unless you concentrate." And she was right. Even at this shrunken size, the machine was big enough to kill.

"*Take prisoners!*" Ben chanted again. And once more he focused on that bottle with all the energy he had; in fact, he thought his chest would burst with the pushed wish of it.

The bottle belted out more heat. He saw the darkness ripple as the digger hurtled toward them. This time it dwindled to the size of a vehicle on a toddlers' fairground ride.

From behind he heard the witch call out, "Take it easy. Don't break a leg!"

Ben ached to turn. He wanted to find out what the witch had meant, but he couldn't look — not then — because the next zap of power was fizzling around the digger, shrinking it to the size of a toy.

The sengi leaped to the ground. The machine hesitated. Its tiny wheels spun in the mud as if its driver sought to retreat. Before there was any chance of that, the sengi fiercely chased it onward to Ben. All he had to do was bend and scoop it into the neck of the bottle. Then he tipped the bottle upright. And jammed in the stopper, tight.

The Watercow

CHAPTER 35

With a shout, Ben held the bottle high. He turned in triumph — and saw Mom sitting on the ground, looking bewildered. As for the witch and the beetle, they were tiny again. They were back inside their eggshell, and they were dancing. The shell was smaller too. It appeared about the size of a chicken's egg, and it was spinning.

Ben sprang toward it. He guessed that they were leaving, and there were things he wanted to ask, things he wanted to say — he wanted to thank them. But as he approached, the eggshell swiveled more swiftly, as if it were joining the witch's dance, and soon the wind seemed to waltz along with them, wrapping them up, whisking them away.

Only the witch's voice floated back: "Good times are a-coming next. There'll be a break in this weather, and the watercow should manage the rest."

"What do you know about the watercow?" demanded Ben.

There was no answer. With those last riddling words, they had gone.

Ben turned to Mom. "I never even thanked them," he said. It was only then that he realized that she was hurt. "Mom, what's wrong?"

"It's OK—I've just twisted my ankle." She was trying to smile, though her voice was all wobbly. "I can't believe it: first I'm rescued from a flood, then as soon as I'm back on shore, I manage to injure myself. I'm such an idiot. I'm too old to spin—that's all. It made me dizzy. And when I saw what happened to Pike—I'm sorry, Ben, but it gave me such a shock that I fell over. I don't like to think you can just get rid of people like that. That bottle of yours is horrible."

"It's not my bottle," said Ben. He was feeling shaken himself. "But it's a good thing I had it, isn't it?" He looked at it dubiously. "Maybe we could take it to the police station."

"And let them open it? That'd be interesting."

Ben helped her up. They needed to move. The water was creeping onto the land.

"I'm sorry, Ben, I'll have to go slowly," she said, wincing. "I think you should go on ahead and raise the alarm."

Ben thrust the bottle into his pocket and darted around to her injured side. "I'm not leaving you!" he said firmly. "We're staying together."

So they hobbled from tussock to tussock. The tough, scrubby grass rose and fell like mermaid hair as they struggled onward. Mud sucked at their feet, foam gurgled, and rain and wind blasted their faces.

The sengi's soaked fur was plastered to her skull — she looked half drowned. Ben lifted her from his shoulder into his pocket. She didn't protest, though she did demand that they keep moving. "Once we're away from the bank, we'll find Flummery," she squeaked. "Or the bees will find him first. After that we'll see to this flooding, and then —"

Mom interrupted, wearily shaking her head. "I don't think there's any chance we'll find him."

The sengi became taut with anguish. "Don't underestimate the bees," she cried. "They're finders. They found everyone tonight: they found you; they found Ben; they'll find Flummery. They have to!" She broke off then to stuff her tail between her teeth. Ben saw that she quivered in distress. Tears pricked his own eyes too as he remembered those monstrous wheels that had flattened the mud where the owl fell.

"D'you think the bees might find Dad's stone?" he asked with an extra pang.

"Your dad's stone?" wailed Mom. "Oh Ben, you haven't lost that — it was very special."

"Of course it was special. That's why Flummery had it," Ben

said fiercely. "It was more special than you know. I don't think it really belonged to Dad or me."

"What d'you mean?"

As they stumbled toward the museum, Ben told Mom about the watercow. He thought that a story might be a good way of distracting her from the pain. But when he reached the end of the tale, Mom said, "So you think it's the  same stone? Oh, I think you might be disappointed, Ben. I don't think it's any sort of diamond — it looked like a bit of worn glass to me."

"What if you're wrong?" Ben was defiant. "What if the captain found the watercow before he died? What if he brought it back here? He always said he would. I bet Montgomery found the diamond. I bet he took it when he went away. I think that's why Dad ended up having it."

The sengi had listened, silent and quivering, but now she shook her head. "That's impossible. No watercow was ever at the museum. Ask the hippo," she said. "He would know if one had arrived with him in that final shipment. I know his memory's a disgrace, but he wouldn't have forgotten if he'd traveled with a watercow."

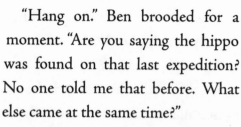

"Hang on." Ben brooded for a moment. "Are you saying the hippo was found on that last expedition? No one told me that before. What else came at the same time?"

"Nothing important." The sengi shrugged. "I wasn't in the room where they unpacked the crates, but there were very few. The expedition was cut short when the captain fell ill. All he brought back was the hippo, and a pair of duikers, and a mongoose. Oh, and a box of rare butterflies. Those drew a lot of attention at the time."

"I'd like to see the butterflies," said Mom. She sounded tired. Ben could tell she was trying to prevent more squabbling.

"You will see them," he promised. "You'll see everything when we get there, and you'll love it."

And then he went quiet himself, because the mystery of the watercow was dancing in his tired head like a butterfly beyond his reach. The answer seemed almost within his grasp when Mom interrupted his thoughts: "Hey, there's a light over there. Somebody's coming."

She was right.

"It must be the police at last!" she exclaimed.

She was excited.

So was Ben.

Yet there was something odd about that light. It approached from a strange direction. And it moved with a curious lilt. Soon they knew it was far too bright to be a flashlight.

"It's a searchlight," declared Mom.

But it was in the wrong place to be a searchlight. And it was growing overwhelmingly bright: a bluish, sparkling white, too intense to be faced head-on. They flinched from that blinding brilliance as it bathed the river and the mud and every blade of grass in a shining liquid silver. Yet still the light drew nearer, and nearer, and nearer, so that they could watch it only obliquely as it moved upriver.

Presently the reflections from the water revealed that a giant beast moved behind the light. It was hard to determine how large this creature could be. Buffalo-size, perhaps? Or elephant-size? They hardly cared, for the biggest surprise was the light itself — it was blazing from the creature's open mouth.

The great beast hesitated. Slowly, almost carefully, it closed its jaws, giving them a glimpse of tusklike teeth before all that remained of the light was a glowing smile. Poor Mom stifled a cry. For now that the light had gone, the night had never seemed so black, and as far as she was concerned, here was a creature the size of a car between them and the shore. Yet even as she moved to protect Ben, he gave a shout of delight.

He had felt a touch of velvet energy. And all of a sudden, the pieces of the watercow mystery snapped into place in his mind as he realized that this huge creature was somehow also the hippo. But now the hippo appeared to be the larger size that Ben had so often sensed. As for the light that blazed from his mouth — what else could it be but the missing diamond?

The Diamond

CHAPTER 36

"You're telling me this is another one of your friends?" exclaimed Mom as the hippo approached.

"Yes, I think so," said Ben. He could tell Mom was trying to be calm, but she wasn't succeeding.

"You said it was a pygmy hippo."

"He was smaller last time I saw him."

"I see." But plainly she did not "see" at all, for abruptly she added, "Ben, I'm confused. What is it? A hippo or a watercow?"

"I am both," declared the hippo. His voice was muffled, as though he had something large in his mouth.

"*You're both!*" the sengi snapped. "All this time and you never bothered to *mention* it?"

"I had forgotten."

"How could you forget something *so* important?"

The hippo said quite simply, "I was forgetful because I'd lost and forgotten an important part of myself."

Ben hardly listened because he had spotted a black shadow

against the dazzling cave of the hippo's mouth. It was an owl-shaped shadow — Flummery's shadow, in fact.

"Oh my lord, that thing has eaten the owl," wailed Mom.

"I'm not eaten. But I can't come out," Flummery said. "Every time I try, he starts to shrink to his normal size. And if he did that we'd be swept away in this flood."

"It's true," said the hippo vaguely. "I have no control over my size."

"This is crazy," cried Mom, head in her hands.

"I think that stone Ben put around my neck is the cause of it," said the owl.

"Of course it is," said Ben. "I thought you'd guessed it was the diamond. Why didn't you take it off and give it to the hippo properly?"

The owl's outline grew ruffled. In fact, he sounded rather offended. "I couldn't undo it. You'd tied the knot too tight. Anyway, you told me to give it to Constance."

"Whyever did you fly into his mouth in the first place?" asked Mom. She was looking more baffled by the minute.

The hippo was the one who explained. "The bees guided me to meet you," he said. "I was late. But I waited. As a matter of fact I was waiting in the wrong place, on the other side of the ridge, when that digger appeared and Flummery came bowling out of it. Actually I think I made a rather neat catch —"

"With his mouth," the owl broke in.

"Though I caught rather more than I expected, and then this happened."

"And when I came to, I was in his mouth and the digger had vanished."

"Let me tell you," said the hippo, "we have both had quite a shock."

"So have we all," said Mom with a lot of feeling.

The hippo moved alongside them. He was massive.

Mom took a deep loud breath and held it in as Ben reached toward the owl, meaning to help him with the stone. "Ben, you're not to go near its mouth!" she cried. "It could bite your arm off."

"I wouldn't," said the hippo mildly. "I'm a vegetarian."

"We can trust him," Ben assured her. Then, whether his mom liked it or not, he stepped nearer to that blinding diamond-saturated light. He had to close his eyes as he felt for the stone and tried to undo the wet knots. He couldn't fidget. He had to concentrate hard. However, this had the benefit of focusing his mind, and he began to think more clearly about the diamond too.

It had to be magic, didn't it?

That meant there might be some magic words — simple

instructions, the witch had said — yet he'd need to say them with all his heart. He thought about that. He asked himself if he was truly ready to let the diamond go. Wasn't it all he'd ever had that belonged to his dad? Then, with a rush, he realized that the whole museum belonged to Dad's family and that they were his family too. As he teased the last tight loop from the soggy leather, he knew what the words should be.

The diamond fell into his hand. With a great flap, the owl burst free while Ben dropped Dad's stone onto the hippo's tongue and whispered, "Take back what's yours, but please, if you can, use it to save our museum." And he spoke those words with every drop of meaning he could muster. Then he withdrew.

After that the hippo closed his mouth. He gulped. It was a loud gulp. A whale might have swallowed more quietly. He followed the gulp with a belch loud enough to make a dragon blush. Yet the hippo merely smiled, and the upturned line of his satisfaction lit the waterside.

"Now I feel strong. Now I can think quite clearly," he declared.

"Maybe," said the sengi dryly, "but how long do you intend to stay at that ridiculous size?"

"I can choose any size I want, now that the diamond has been returned to me," replied the hippo. "But I think this is a good size for carrying you all home to the museum."

"You're joking," said Mom. "I'm not getting up there."

But the hippo wasn't joking. Besides, Mom had no other choice, because all this time, the river had been rising and they were cut off. They now stood on a little island.

Eventually all four were seated on the hippo's back. It had been a tough scramble for Mom; indeed, no one was finding it comfortable. This was because the hippo was now so wide that afterward Ben said it was like riding a table — a polished, giant, hippo-shaped table. Nevertheless, the hippo's gait was wonderfully smooth, for he was built to move in rivers, so the suck of the mud and the turbulence of the currents were no trouble for him. He thrust his way through the water in a path of light from his diamond smile, while the sengi teetered by his ear, squeaking directions, and soon, despite the danger, everyone felt more cheerful.

Even the rain seemed gentler then, quick and soft, edging toward a drizzle. Only as they approached the museum did their faces grow grim again — for they saw the extent of the flooding. The rising water was meandering over the land, pool joining pool, a shining skin as far as they could see.

Flummery became very restless. "I can't roost here all night," he said. "I'll fly up ahead and ask the bees how it looks inside, then I'll meet you by the front door."

"You mean you'll find out if it's flooded in there?" called Mom. "Isn't it bound to be?"

"I'll discover all I can," the owl promised as he glided away.

"Tell Constance we're coming," said Ben.

"Yes, say we'll be right behind you," cried Mom.

"As soon as we've fixed this flooding," added Ben.

"No." Mom shook her head. "Ben, that's going to take a lot of people and some big machines."

"But we can't wait for that," he insisted. "I bet the hippo could do something."

In answer the hippo swung into the wind and opened his mouth wide. The weir became decked in diamond light, and amid the churning reflections they could see the wedged tree. It certainly blocked the weir. Worse, a barricade of branches and flotsam had built up against it and was forming a glittering tangled dam that stretched all the way to the shore. It was causing the river to seek a new path overland.

Mom was deadly serious now. "There's nothing we can do here," she declared. "This is worse than I thought. If the flood's reached the building, we've got to get Miss Garner-Gee out and call the emergency services."

"And leave all this?" gasped Ben.

"We have to. It's dangerous even to be near it."

"But he's the watercow. He should be able to do something."

The hippo turned and inquired, "Like what? Do you have any suggestions?"

"Well . . ." Ben squirmed in despair. "I . . . I don't care how you do it, but you've got the diamond now, so can't you magic it all away? I don't know . . . blow at it or something?"

"I had not thought of that," the hippo said thoughtfully. "Before I try, you had all better hold on tight."

And lucky they did, for almost at once his ribs began to expand, and with an enormous yawn of light, he blew.

277

The Watercow's Breath

CHAPTER 37

Ben said afterward that it was like being seated on the back of the wind. The breath of the watercow rolled back the river until it gathered in a huge silver wave — a wall of water that mounted higher, and then higher still, until it seemed that it would dash over them and drown the whole city.

Mom yelled, "What are you doing?"

Ben snatched up the sengi so she wouldn't be swept away. And still the hippo blew. They glimpsed fish rising to the surface like flashing pewter plates amid the silver spray as the wave grew and grew; soon it seemed to hang against the sky, balancing for impossible seconds . . . until at last, with a great booming crash, it collapsed atop the tree and the broken bridge. It flushed everything over the weir — the tree and the tangled detritus all tumbled together into the torrent below and were broken up by the force of the falls and carried away.

The backwash was immense. Ben was leaning forward now, flat on his tummy, arms clasped around the hippo's neck. Mom clung tightly behind him as their world became a tossing expanse of roaring brown and silver, which foamed and spread and threatened to sweep everything away. They felt the sting of water on their faces. They smelled its oily reek as it broke from the horizontal plain, rearing to swallow the sky. Yet the hippo stood house-solid, seeming suddenly huge — a giant in the woods; indeed, for a giddy instant Ben thought he saw into the startled nests of the rooks. Then, as the river swirled and seethed and sucked its substance back into itself, the hippo turned and headed inland through the trees.

Ben hadn't thought about the mist for hours. He had been too frantic. Too tired. Now, though, as the hippo plodded along the length of the building, the idea of going inside made his stomach churn.

Mom was aware of his drooping. "Tired?" she said. "Not much longer now. Once we're in there, we'll phone the police and it'll soon be over."

"They're not going to be much use at sorting out the mist," Ben muttered.

Mom sighed impatiently. "What's the problem with the mist?" she asked. "I wish you'd stop hinting and tell me what you're worried about. I know you said the witch conjured it, but wasn't she a good witch?"

The sengi was biting her tail again. "The witch didn't start off so obliging," she said darkly.

"The witch was angry when she summoned the mist," the hippo explained. "It's wild magic. So afterward she had no real control of it, and it's very unpredictable. All we know is that by now it will have permeated everything, so size will make no difference to what it might choose to animate."

"So not just small things like insects," said Ben.

The hippo sighed. "I don't mean to alarm you," he said. "If you do see anything surprising, it will merely be an echo from another time. And those aren't so very unusual. Fainter echoes of memories and thoughts can be found in most old buildings if you listen in the shadows."

Mom laughed nervously. "I think I'd call that the atmosphere of the building."

"Exactly. It's the same thing," said the hippo eagerly. "The point is that this mist can manipulate the strongest of those memories. They may come close enough for you to be aware of them in time present. But that is all. They cannot cause you any harm."

"Couldn't your diamond stop the mist?" asked Ben.

"I have been thinking about that," said the hippo. "But the diamond amplifies magic, so if I'm not careful, it might make the mist more powerful."

"It's a pity the mist can't protect the museum from this flooding," said Mom.

"I'm thinking about that too," said the hippo gravely.

The sengi was grooming her whiskers. She appeared to be tying them in knots. "So am I," she said. "The flood is the worst worry of all for us."

"It's true," said the hippo. "That's because it's real. River damage is serious. Anything this flood penetrates may rot and decay, and if that happens, it would be a permanent change. It could be ruinous."

"Well, let's get in there and see how bad it is," said Mom. "Are the doors unlocked?"

"No, but Leon will open them for us," said the hippo.

"And Flummery might have some news from the bees," said Ben as they rounded the corner to the front of the museum.

"But where is he?" squeaked the sengi. "I don't see him."

"We can't wait," Mom insisted. She was gazing at the water, which had reached the front steps. "We just can't. Look at this flooding. If I'd known he wasn't going to be here, I'd have insisted we use the back door. I must check on Miss Garner-Gee.

She's old. And if there really is mist and water in there, she might have fallen. I know I'm not much use with this ankle, but I've got to get in there right away. I feel responsible."

"Constance is more capable than you imagine," said the hippo calmly. "But I agree. We ought to join her. Ben, perhaps you could dismount. I'll have to return to my usual size to fit through those doors."

Ben was glad to stretch his legs. He slithered down, splashing like a brick into the water — although here, near the road, it was only ankle-deep.

"Maybe Flummery's around by the hive," he suggested. "I'll check." He splashed around the corner to the hive entrance. It was silent and dark. Nothing moved. "He's not here," he called back.

"Wait!" The sengi raised her head, and her nose gyrated vigorously. "I'm sure he's close by: I can smell him. I think he might be in that thicket." She whisked to Ben's shoulder, indicating some bushes that blocked their view of the road.

Ben saw nothing.

"Hurry up!" Mom cried. "The doors are opening."

When Ben turned to join them, the hippo and Mom were already mounting the steps. The hippo was back to his normal size, and both were partly obscured by the mist that was drifting from the open door. It swelled. And it spread. And it

glowed with a faint greenish phosphorescence. Ben smelled its gluey scent, and his skin pricked into goose bumps. And he faltered, because he felt full of dread.

Out of the blue, a car turned a corner, heading toward the museum. The hippo had reached the top of the steps, so he hastened inside. If he hadn't, he would have been caught in those headlights and seen. But Ben's instinct was to spring into the shadow of the wall, and before he could change his mind, the doors had closed. When the headlights swept over the museum, no one was on the steps. But Ben was still outside, shivering in the shadows. He couldn't believe he had been left behind.

The car passed.

"Well, that wasn't clever," said the sengi. "Still, I don't suppose anyone saw you, and Leon will open up as soon as he can."

They watched the doors expectantly.

They didn't open.

The sengi chewed her tail. Then she began to untie the knots in her whiskers. "Maybe we'd better find Flummery first," she suggested. And she added quite kindly, "Don't worry. You've still got me."

Ben guessed she was nervous too, so he tried to swallow his tears. The car must have turned down a side road. The only sounds now were some early traffic rumbling over the bridge and birdsong. The birds sounded expectant and excited: it really was almost dawn. The black sky was softening to indigo. Soon there would be more people around, going to work, going to school.

And he had been up all night! Hadn't he always wanted to stay up all night?

He sniffed. "OK, let's find Flummery," he said, and tried to sound brisk and cheery. He took a big breath through his nose and waded toward the thicket. Now that the clouds were lifting, the air was a bracing cold that almost hurt — like sucking an extra-strong peppermint — yet it made him feel alert. When he breathed out, he was surrounded by his own frosty breath. He blew the biggest breath clouds he could and wished that he were some sort of dragon that could defeat mists and floods and all enemies of the museum.

"Do behave yourself," said the sengi. "I think I heard … yes … there's Flummery. Look!"

Before she'd finished squeaking, the air seemed a-tumble with an anxious buzzing and a flustering of wings.

Flummery hooted, "Quick! Back to the museum!"

"What? Why?"

"Your bikes have been spotted. You left them where anyone could see them, and *she* did. Hurry!"

Then he and the bees were gone, and Ben heard someone running, splashing toward them, and, in a tizzy himself, he supposed that it could be the police, and what would they think if they saw him out so early?

"Move!" screeched the sengi, diving into Ben's hood.

Because it wasn't the police.

Unexpected Visitors

CHAPTER 38

It was Tara Snow. She saw Ben just as he saw her. "You?" she yelped. "I knew I'd seen that bike before. Why are you here?"

Ben bolted.

She followed fast — surprisingly so. He could hear her splashing; she seemed to be right on his heels. He didn't pause to look back; he simply raced for the doors.

Flummery was already there, fluttering against them like a giant moth as he screeched for Leon. Nonetheless, it seemed an age before the doors opened and the owl and the bees swept indoors. In spite of the billowing mist, Ben was more than eager to follow. He took the steps two at a time.

But so did she. "Have you seen Mr. Pike?" she demanded — so close behind that he could see the cold cloud of her breath.

Dodging, he lunged at the doors, hoping to slam them in her face, but she grabbed him before he could do so and her fingernails dug into his collarbone as she shunted him inside.

"Let me go!" he shouted. "LET. ME. GO!" He fought now, pumping with his elbows, struggling, butting with his head.

"Stop it! What are you doing?" she shrieked as he kicked her in the shins. It was no good; she was gripping him so tightly that he could smell her sickly sweet scent.

Then the door slammed, trapping them both, and in the dark turmoil that followed, Ben felt something scuttle onto his shoulders. It was the chameleon. Even at this distance, Ben could scarcely distinguish Leon's gray-green camouflaged skin from the rest of their surroundings. But he had felt him.

And so had Tara Snow. She shuddered. "Ugh, what was that?"

"I don't know what you're talking about," Ben lied as Leon slipped under the collar of his coat.

Luckily, that was when she looked around the room, then swore and went abruptly still. Ben stopped struggling too. He was almost as startled as she was by what had happened to the lobby.

It ought to have been pitch-dark in there, yet pinpricks of green were reflecting on the flooded floor where, instead of flagstones underfoot, there was a soft stickiness, like mud on the bottom of a pond. Something dripped from overhead onto the surface of the water. As for the mist, it had changed in consistency since Ben was last inside: it was thinner, hotter, jungle-steamy, and it shifted constantly, so that when he looked up to see the source of the dripping, he glimpsed a multitude of tiny lights pulsing in turquoise and green and blue.

"Glowworms," whispered Leon, hushed and tickle-close to Ben's ear.

Almost at the same moment, Tara Snow said, "It's the boiler. That explains all this smoke. You should be glad you're with me. You'd better do as you're told now — boilers can be very dangerous."

Ben turned in astonishment. "Boiler?"

She nodded arrogantly. "I wondered about it yesterday afternoon when I saw all that steam. It's clearly malfunctioning."

The sengi squirmed inside his collar. "Typical," she whispered. "People so often pay no heed to what they think is impossible. It makes them feel safer."

Ben stared. How could this woman ignore what was all around them? Couldn't she hear the rustle of birds, the flutter of lizards, and the scampering of tiny creatures? Nearby, insects buzzed and swarmed; bats skimmed by, stirring the air with their leathery wings; frogs plopped in and out of the water. He looked at Tara Snow with scorn.

Actually, she must have been at least half aware of something, for abruptly she cried, "My God, I think there's some sort of infestation too. It could be rats coming in from the river."

"Don't you like rats?" Ben said slyly.

She turned on him then. "*You're* a little rat. I bet you've got something to do with this smoke."

"I haven't!" shouted Ben. "How could I? You must be blind if you can't see that this is magic. And it's not going to let you get this museum no matter how much you try."

He regretted this outburst at once.

"Magic!" she sneered. Then she went silent, but he could tell it was a thinking-hard, plotting sort of silence. Abruptly she gave a bitter half-laugh. "You're the long-lost cousin, aren't you? Why didn't I guess that before?" Then her fingernails gripped him so hard that he wanted to cry out. "And you've been meddling," she hissed. "You and that old woman have somehow done this out of spite. I don't know how, but believe me, I'm going to find out."

"No! How could I? I didn't. I —"

She caught him midsentence by the throat. "Oh, you are in *such* trouble," she snarled, and her long bony forearm wrapped his collar in an elbow-lock so tight that he could hardly breathe. He wondered if she might strangle him, and he worried that the sengi and Leon might be squashed, until he felt them shrink into the gap at the nape of his neck.

The sengi crept up behind his right ear, and in the tiniest of

289

whispers, she advised him to go limp. "Predators loosen their grip when you do," she explained. "It puts them off guard."

Leon slunk up to his other ear and rasped, "Your mother and the hippo had to hurry to help Constance. Flummery has joined them too. They left *me* to keep an eye on you. First we need to get you free of this woman. But that won't be hard. She stinks of fear. Soon she'll make a mistake. Be ready to fly the moment she does."

"She's only holding you with one arm now," the sengi reported from his other side. "She's taking out her phone. She thinks she can hold you while she makes a call."

"I'm ready," murmured Ben, hardly moving his mouth or making a sound.

However, as it turned out, he wasn't as ready as he'd thought. Tara Snow didn't make a call. Instead there was a sudden *flash!* and a moment's shock of vivid blinding green as a photographic light flooded the room. Then the next second, the room was pitch-black again.

Ben gritted his teeth. That would have been such an excellent moment to run. Had he missed his chance? He hoped she would take more pictures.

"I'm getting a record of this," said Tara Snow. "This place is a health and safety hazard, and I'm going to report it. No one's going to pretend this didn't happen."

"Sometimes photos don't come out," Ben said slyly.

"One of them will. I'm going to take plenty," she said, fiddling with her phone.

"Are you ready?" whispered the sengi.

"Ready," Ben said in a tiny voice from the side of his mouth.

"Ready with tooth and claw?" breathed Leon.

Here it came: *flash!*

Then they all attacked: Leon and the sengi leaped at the woman's pointed face while Ben kicked backward like a wild pony and bit her arm really hard!

Tara Snow shrieked. Shocked by the attack and blinded by her own photoflash, she ever so briefly slackened her grasp. It was enough. Ben wrenched free and sprang away, crossing the soft, flooded floor with tremendous splashing leaps. But when he entered the egg room, all the glowworms went out altogether.

"There's no point in running away," Tara Snow yelled from the darkness. "This building isn't safe, and anyway you're trespassing. I've already called the police."

"You're the trespasser," Ben called back over his shoulder. "We'll tell them what you've done — you and Mr. Pike."

"Julian? Have you seen Julian? I've been looking for him. Is he already here?" Panic rose in her voice.

This time Ben stayed silent. He was pretty sure the mist was clotting and changing again, but for once he welcomed the

milky feel of it against his skin because it was hiding him.

He waded away from the place where she had last heard him as quietly as he could. He hoped to find the hallway entrance and escape through it before she caught up with him. From the random sound of her splashes, he guessed that the inky darkness was confusing her too. He was feeling confused himself, because by now he ought to have come across the egg cabinet. Indeed the shape of the room seemed changed beyond recognition. He felt lost.

Suddenly he was startled by a sound on his left, soft as a moth's wing. Then he sensed as much as saw a smutty black plume of deeper dark against the bruise-gray, which gradually formed into the shape of two figures. They seemed to be talking quietly, and though Ben couldn't hear what they said, he was struck by a dreamlike notion that he had watched these same two murmuring figures once before, and for some reason, instead of being frightened, he longed to be within the vague soft sphere of their presence.

They walked. He followed, the thought of losing them making him feel bereft, though he couldn't have said why. Not until the moment when the taller of the two turned and beckoned.

"Dad?" Ben whispered.

The Pufferfish and the Ark

CHAPTER 39

The figures merged into the blackness, but to Ben's surprise, the entrance to the hallway was right in front of him. No wonder he'd missed it before: it had transformed. It looked more like a cave, a very slimy sort of cave, the sort that would be better to avoid because of what might live there.

The mist drifting over the entrance slowly pulsed, giving the moss-covered walls the appearance that they were breathing. Indeed, they smelled alive. Nevertheless, he knew this was his best hope of escape — and besides, he thought, Dad had gone in that direction . . . if it really *had* been his dad. Slipping inside the murky, dank passage, he wondered whether he had imagined it.

The water grew deeper every few steps. Before long it went over his shins. Then it was over his knees. Presently he passed a patch of fluorescent fungi that glimmered a ghoulish, sickly green, like the numbers on an alarm clock. Before long, he noticed these glowing fungi patches appeared regularly on both sides, and he decided that they marked the side doors.

To his surprise, when he glanced back, he could see only sooty darkness. The fungi that lit his path had faded away after he passed.

Somewhere behind, he could hear Tara Snow splashing after him. Yet she sounded farther and farther away. Strange thoughts occurred to Ben then. Could the hallway be helping him—and hindering Tara Snow? Maybe the doors were sealed by this fungus too. If so, could the fungus be preventing the water from flooding the side rooms?

While he was considering all this, he saw, to his great relief, a patch of gray that must mark the end of the hall. Then he glimpsed the couple again. They were walking ahead of him. This time he made out the woman more clearly, and it seemed to him then that she was much the older of the two. It could have been Constance Garner-Gee, except that her bearing was more upright— like someone ten years younger.

295

He hastened toward them. He wanted to run, but he was nervous of making too much noise. Yet, as the light grew to a swarthy greenish-gray, their outline became vague as a smudge and faded altogether by the time he reached the atrium. He was quite alone as he stepped out of the darkness into a viridian predawn light. He halted there. He was astounded all over again.

The floor of the courtyard was the lowest part of the museum, so he wasn't surprised to find that the flooding was deepest in there. Yet there was so much water. It stretched as far as he could see, and it steamed and bubbled like a vast volcanic pool surrounded by huge growths of putrid puffballs, strident tropical ferns, and lush species of vines bearing massive rubbery leaves. The boundaries of the room were indistinct, far away, lost in shadows and mist, and as Ben edged forward, the metal pillars that supported the roof appeared to move too, softly sliding around the sides of his vision, rising like tree trunks to the creeper-covered ceiling where the wrought-iron beams crisscrossed the glass. Up there the beams looked more like branches because they were festooned with giant violet flowers amid a canopy of twining tendrils. As far as Ben could see in this deep green-gray, the animals that were usually displayed in the courtyard had vanished.

Some way forward — far, far distant, it seemed — he noticed a mound that sloped from the water and disappeared into the canopy. The mist in between quivered, as the air does in a long-shot wildlife film, but all the same Ben thought he detected some movement on the mound. There was no chance he could reach it though, not with this vast stretch of bubbling water blocking his way. He felt terribly lonely.

He wondered where Mom was. Where were the hippo and Flummery, and the others? He had expected to see them all here. Yet there was no one. There was hardly a movement in the air. Not a sound. He couldn't even hear Tara Snow anymore.

Which way should he go? There wasn't much choice because deeper water spread everywhere except at the edge of the room where he stood. He slunk left, along the wall, where the water reached halfway up his thighs. Soon he had to thrust through some vegetation that looked like a scaly wet feather duster. It gave way with a delicate brushing sensation as if it weren't entirely there.

As he sidled through it, step by jungle step, his attention kept sliding to a particularly murky area across the water. He didn't remember it being there when he had first left the hall, but now, amid the wraiths and streams of mist, a shadow appeared to be drifting. At first he saw no form to the shadow, only an occasional flicker of light that swung out in a pendular motion, then disappeared inside.

There it went . . . out and up, then back again.

Something about the shape of that light was familiar.

He held his breath, waiting.

There it came — out and up — but this time, before it swung back, he recognized it. He was watching the pufferfish lantern. It was lighting the way for a dull metal shadow-ship that floated behind it. The ship was revealed slowly to Ben, inch, by inch, by inch, and he had time to wonder why it looked so familiar. He couldn't think where he'd seen it.

All that time it grew lighter. It became light enough to see that the ship had passengers on board. First he spotted the unmistakable shape of a giraffe, then squinting hard, he discerned there were more: the zebra and the polar bear were there, and so were the moose and the kangaroo, and a huge snake and a flock of assorted birds perched on the mast. This ship was acting like an ark. It was filled with all manner of animal refugees from the flood. But truly that was only the beginning of the strangeness that night, for every now and then Ben glimpsed a human figure working among that menagerie.

Constance Garner-Gee was captaining the ship. Upright and serene she was, standing as if she were accustomed to sailing through mist and magic in the middle of the night. He watched her stretch to reach a monkey that hung awkwardly from a vine. She seemed to be persuading it to join them. Sure enough, the monkey bounded to her shoulder, then leaped to join the rest. Meanwhile the pufferfish swung higher as if it were encouraging a baboon family that was perched a little farther ahead. They looked nervous, but in the end they jumped aboard.

Ben scanned the ship desperately, hoping to see Dad on board with Constance. He wanted to call out to her, yet he felt strangely shy as he raised his hand. As he hesitated, the ship veered away toward the distant mound. And at that same moment the water immediately in front of Ben began to swirl violently.

With a jolt he saw that something was under there.

No shadow, this. It was something real and solid, and his heart hammered then, for the thing was about to break the surface very close by. He thought of the creatures he had seen in the lobby. This was larger than any of those, and his mind ran to sea monsters.

When the hippo's ears broke through the water, Ben gave a bleat of relief.

"Sorry," the hippo said as his whole head emerged. "Did I alarm you? I could see you'd spotted Constance. You mustn't interrupt her, though. There's so little time to rescue so many; everyone must be safely out of the water and onto higher ground before dawn. It's possible the mist may leave us then, but the flood will stay until . . ."

"What d'you mean 'higher ground'?" said Ben, impatient and gruff, because the hippo was talking as if nothing unusual were happening at all. "What have you done with my mom? I thought you'd be looking after her." The hippo lumbered onto his plinth — though the plinth was underwater too, so when he'd settled, he was still flank-deep in the flood. He took his time. Ben was almost jumping with impatience before the hippo replied, "The staircase and the mezzanine level are our high ground. Never you worry — your mother is safely up there. I'm more concerned about those who remain at floor level."

Ben looked at the mound again. Now that he knew what it was, he could see the rough shape of the staircase. It was simply that swathes of vegetation were hiding the structure underneath. And there were creatures on the stairs too. But no sign of Mom.

All at once a shape broke away from the rest and came flapping toward them at speed. It was Flummery.

Time Past and Time Present

CHAPTER 40

Ahead of them was a moss-buried stump that appeared to flourish fungi the size of an elephant's ear. This was where Flummery landed. When Ben started forward, anxious for news, he realized that the stump was actually the gramophone pedestal. In this mist, everything looked so different. It was very alarming.

"Careful!" warned the hippo. "Watch for the steps."

Luckily Ben heard him and paid attention. The steps leading down to the sunken courtyard were hidden underwater, so if he hadn't halted, he'd have taken a tumble.

This was such a small incident, yet Ben felt suddenly overwhelmed.

301

"What's the matter, Ben?" the hippo said softly.

Ben was silent for a moment. Then he admitted, "I think I saw my dad!"

The hippo sighed. "I thought you might have."

"He showed me the entrance to the hall when I was lost," said Ben. "Will I see him again?"

"I think you simply saw your own memory," the hippo said. "Didn't that memory of your father draw you here in the first place?"

"No, it was more than that." Ben violently shook his head. But then his shoulders sank as he realized that the vision of Dad had actually been exactly like a part of that childhood memory.

The owl sidled to the edge of the stump. "It's a good, strong memory that is part of you," he said. "Did you see anyone else?"

"Yes. I saw Constance," mumbled Ben. Then more lucidly he added, "First I thought I saw her with Dad. But then she was on that boat with the pufferfish. She was getting the animals to jump inside. I suppose she was rescuing them from the water, but I don't understand how —"

The hippo interrupted him: "I doubt Constance understands herself," he said. "No one understands wild magic, but yesterday, after meeting you, she was determined to save this museum in any way she could."

"It took great courage," added the owl, "even with the pufferfish's help."

At that Ben gave a gasp. "I knew I'd seen that ship before. I saw it in the office. The pufferfish called it the Little Ship of Venice. But it was small. It would have fit in my hand!"

"It's one of Constance's favorites," said the owl, shaking the mist from his wings. "It was made for measuring time, though when Constance was your age, she liked to imagine sailing in it."

The hippo nodded. "When the mist stirred that memory, Constance had the courage to seize the past and use it to save the animals."

The owl cocked his head at the hippo. "With some help from you, my friend, if I am not mistaken," he said. "Something reinforced that magic to make a daydream ship substantial enough to take passengers."

The hippo didn't deny it. "When Constance prayed for her ship, I wished her success with all my heart," he grunted. "I think the diamond played some part, for I feel rather weary. Yet there's still so much more to be done."

The owl nodded urgently. "Yes, everyone must be out of the water before the mist departs."

"But he's standing right in it!" said Ben, pointing at the hippo.

The hippo winked. "I still have some protection, thanks to you. That being so, I have come to my usual place to greet visitors. I gather we have one."

Ben clapped his hand to his mouth. "I should have said! I let

Tara Snow in here. She was right behind me not so long ago! I couldn't stop her. . . ."

"But you did a grand job of distracting her while the rest of us were busy," said Flummery. "That was valuable time you gave us."

Ben shook his head. "I wasn't trying to distract her. I was just trying to —"

"Never mind," the hippo said. "You did very well. Watch now: the final cargo of animals is disembarking."

This was true. While they had been talking, the pufferfish had guided the ship alongside the overgrown staircase — in the growing light, Ben could see the stairs more clearly. The animals on board were bunching near the prow. He couldn't tell quite how they would disembark because the bulk of the vessel blocked his view, but he saw that the lions were the first to mount the stairs, with an anteater snuffling behind them. The zebra came next. Meanwhile, others that already crowded the stairs shifted upward toward the gallery, making room for the newcomers. Their motion seemed almost dreamlike — indeed, they didn't seem quite awake; Ben saw no squabbling, no pushing, no one trying to eat anyone else. He guessed this was because it was merely a memory of life that moved them. Certainly, as they drifted up the steps, it was as though they walked in their sleep. Yet someone drove them on. And a moment later he saw that it was Mom.

She was already on the stairs. She was standing up — Ben didn't think she should have been standing on her injured ankle — and with just one hand's support from the banister, it was she who was herding the shuffling creatures into sensible order. At first he just felt proud of her. But soon he began to wonder how she was managing all of it on her own. He could see that Constance and the pufferfish were driving the crowd from the base of the stairs, but as they moved upward, Mom was handling both sides of the crowd. Or was she?

The hairs on the back of his neck prickled as it struck him that Mom was moving as if she were working with someone else. When he looked directly at the other side of the staircase, where a second person would naturally be, he saw no one. Yet if he looked straight at Mom, sometimes, from the corner of his eye, he thought he glimpsed a figure. He blinked. Then he tried the trick of staring both at Mom and at nothing (in that he didn't take his eyes from her, but allowed them to drift out of focus), and when he did this, he discerned the other figure at the edge of his vision. Of course, the urge to look directly at it was almost unbearable. He resisted; instead he tried to unfocus his eyes a little more — a bit like you do when you look at a 3-D picture — and like the moment when the 3-D picture pops from the background, Ben abruptly saw the figure more clearly.

It was Dad. Ben was too far away to see his face; rather, he recognized the roll of his dad's gait and the swing of his shoulders as he worked in concert with Mom. As Ben watched, he felt sure that he'd seen the two of them working in partnership at another time, perhaps in a more domestic setting like cleaning up after a meal or unpacking groceries, and he felt quite certain that these particular movements belonged solely to his parents. He didn't know if he was watching some newly unlocked memory of his own or memories that belonged to his mom. He didn't care.

He yearned to swim out to them. Yet he feared that if he broke his unfocused stare even for a moment, Dad would be gone. He wanted to watch for every possible second — indeed, he tried to avoid blinking. But time passed, and a pearly gray dawn came creeping, seeping through the pewter gloom. It melted the memory of Dad like water washing over a stain. Eventually Ben's stinging eyeballs forced him to blink, and for a microsecond after that blink, he thought he perceived six other shadowy figures on the stairs in old-fashioned clothes, and all of them reminded him a little of Dad. But then his treacherous eyes forced another blink. Afterward no shadow of anyone remained.

"You haven't lost him," the hippo said. His eyes were full of pity as he added, "You've recovered a little of your own early memory of your parents."

"And there may be more," said Flummery gently. "After tonight I think your mother will tell you all that she can."

The hippo nodded. "And Constance could tell you about her family—she'd like to."

The owl's amber eyes looked so dark with concern that Ben had to smile. He shook off his anguished feeling of loss and watched Constance climbing the stairs, holding out her hand to his mom. And Mom was smiling too.

Suddenly the hippo flapped his tail, a splash of alarm that jolted them back to the present. "Here comes our uninvited guest," he warned. "Hide!"

Flummery, not for the first time, disobeyed advice and went swooping into the hall. Presently there was a din: a screech from the owl, a cry, a splash, then a curse from Tara Snow. Ben realized that Flummery was giving him hiding time. He scuttled to the wall, burying himself among leaves that were laced with skeins of fungus, moist with gleaming threads.

"Stay hidden," urged the hippo. "Hold still and silent like me."

Almost at once Tara Snow waded into the atrium. She had green ooze smeared across her suit.

Her hair had escaped its neat clip; it hung lankly over her brow. Her face glistened a sweaty pink, and her glasses were crooked, and her makeup slid in panda smudges under her eyes. She looked disheveled. She looked livid. Yet her bulging eyes weren't searching for Ben — she was too busy working the camera on her phone.

She photographed the room again and again, and as she did, she muttered breathily, "This must be a trick. I'm going to find out how they've done it."

The hippo gazed at her. It was light enough for Ben to see the quizzical gleam in his dark-brown eyes. Despite that, he was statue still, all except his mouth, which began to stretch. Slowly, slowly, his mouth widened and spread, and opened, until he was beaming his toothiest hippo boulevard smile.

What the Hippo Ate That Morning

CHAPTER 41

A shaft of dawn sunlight crept through the canopy and shone upon the hippo. Tara Snow's jaw dropped. As she screamed, something astonishing happened.

A thousand mini-rainbows danced to her shriek, crackling around the edges of every leaf, bending and diffusing the mist among the creepers, the ferns, the fungi, the moss, and then all of that magical vegetation melted, disintegrating into spangles and sequins of sunlight until it seemed that none of it had ever been there. The tall windows that had reappeared blazed with fresh dawn white, and at that moment the mist-free museum appeared as vast as an aircraft hangar.

Next instant the walls shunted to the center, telescoping inward until the flooded atrium assumed its old familiar shape. Naturally this meant that the staircase had glided to its proper position too, so that the distance between Mom and Ben narrowed to its proper size. He might have been tempted to dash to her if the space between them hadn't still been flooded. But it was. And the water looked filthy and deep. Besides, there would scarcely have been room for him: the stairs and the mezzanine were crammed full of creatures.

All the same, they showed no sign of life. Indeed, if you imagined how a museum might appear during a flood, if some strong workers had lifted all the exhibits out of danger and stacked them carefully up on the mezzanine level and the stairs: well, that was how it looked.

Except that there were no workers. And there was no ship — it had disappeared. There was only Mom and Constance Garner-Gee standing together at the base of the stairs. In that clear morning light, they looked small and solid and achingly familiar to Ben. He wanted to hug them both and reassure them because they looked so tired, but he could tell they were bracing themselves to deal with the flood next — and with Tara Snow.

She was gathering like an agitated spider to attack what she thought she had found. She sucked in an enormous breath. Then she shrieked, "This is a public building. This is utterly outrageous. You won't get away with it."

Mom made the mistake of laughing. "Get away with what?" she called.

Tara Snow hated to be mocked; she was one of those people who are equally scared and insulted by what they don't understand, so now her face, already green with fear, became distorted with a queer mixture of hate and horrid satisfaction.

"I know what I saw," she snarled. "I've got a record of it all on my phone. Do you people even have a permit for all those wild animals?"

As if everything were perfectly normal, Constance replied, "Good morning, Miss Snow. I really don't know what you mean, but I might equally ask: Do you have a permit to be here at this hour? I certainly didn't invite you."

Tara Snow ignored that. Brandishing her phone, she shrieked, "I've got photos of it all on here. I have no idea how you've pulled off these tricks, but I do know that this building is no fit place for the public. I'm going to show everything to the authorities . . . today . . . and the police — I've already called them and I'll show them too. They'll be on their way. They won't let you continue in this . . . this . . . irresponsible manner."

"Irresponsible? How dare you!" shouted Mom.

Tara Snow began to wade toward the staircase.

"Take care," warned Constance.

The woman leered, her mouth a twisted purple gash. "I'll *take care*. I'll take care that I report everything I've seen. I know the health and safety regulations. This comes under 'dangerous practices.' You'll never open to the public again."

"Dangerous practices?" yelled Mom. "Can't you see we've been flooded, you stupid woman?"

Ben longed to edge away from where he was standing. Now that the vegetation had gone, it wasn't any use as a hiding place; if Tara Snow happened to turn, she'd see him directly. On the other hand, if he moved, she might hear him. Hoping for advice, he glanced at the hippo — in time to see a cluster of bees circuiting the hippo's head before they swept toward the roof. The hippo followed them with his eyes. So did Ben. And his spirit soared with them as he realized where they were headed.

Flummery was perched upon one of the metal beams. And in that bright morning light, Ben saw that he had passengers: the sengi and Leon were riding among his feathers. All three watched Tara Snow with such focused concentration that every movement she made was mirrored in the quick tilting of their heads, as if they were connected to her by a string. The bees hovered beside them as though they were watching and waiting too.

The woman continued to rant. Her eyes glittered in a devious mad way that Ben didn't like at all. She was advancing toward Mom and Constance now, but slowly. And she kept snapping photos as she went.

I should stop her, thought Ben. He was gathering himself to try when the hippo caught his eye and very gently shook his head. And the hippo's eyes seemed to twinkle with glee. Why?

Ben, watching intently, saw where the woman was heading.

312

And then he guessed. He held his breath, watching her feet, waiting, caught up in tension that almost prickled as she took one . . . more . . . step . . . and . . . tumbled on the underwater steps.

Immediately Flummery plummeted.

He smashed into her arm, and Tara Snow pitched backward. She screeched. Yet she managed to grip her phone tight and hold it above the water.

The bees attacked next. There was no need to sting, for her grasp was tenuous enough. Indeed, when Flummery looped back and struck her arm again, the phone slipped from her grasp. It projected outward in a forceful spinning arc, like a slimy bar of soap.

She splashed after it desperately. Flummery was faster, but his talons were never going to capture anything as smooth as the plastic case of a phone.

But he did not need to catch it: lightning-quick, Leon's tongue flicked out like a live lasso and wrapped up the phone, and then, although it was heavy for her, the sengi helped him heave it onto the owl's shoulder.

Floundering in the water, Tara Snow howled, "GIVE. THAT. BACK!"

In answer, the hippo opened his jaws in his widest car-trunk yawn.

She screamed, backing away in terror.

Meanwhile Flummery sped toward the hippo, swooping between his jaws, and at a precisely perfect moment, the sengi dropped the phone so that it landed neatly on the hippo's tongue.

Tara Snow lurched onto her knees, up to her neck in filthy water, hand over mouth in horror. Perhaps she thought the hippo might eat her. Instead he closed his jaws and gazed at her steadily.

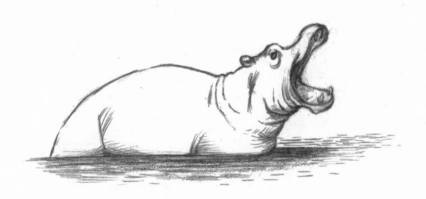

While he gazed, he crunched the cell phone between his teeth. Then he gently spat the pieces back at her.

She staggered back. "Keep that monster away from me," she shrieked — she was hysterical. "I knew it had moved. That's what happened to Julian, isn't it? That thing ate him!"

"No, he didn't," said Ben loudly. "He wouldn't harm anyone."

Tara Snow swiveled around and stared at Ben. Like a desperate crab, she scrambled backward on her hands and feet up the flooded steps, toward him. She looked so wretchedly undignified that Ben felt almost embarrassed. He wondered if he ought to help her up.

"Ben, stay away from her," warned Mom. "She's nuts."

"We haven't even seen Mr. Pike," said Constance.

"I have," said Mom. "Last time I saw him, he'd just finished blocking the weir. He caused this flood, and then he tried to kill us — and I bet *she* knew all about it."

Tara Snow turned on Mom. Drops of saliva flew from her mouth as she insisted, "That's preposterous. That's—" And then there was rowdy chaos as all the women's voices clashed, until Ben covered his ears because he hated it when grown-ups shouted at one another.

Sometimes, though, when you cover your ears, it actually makes it easier to hear. That is why Ben heard the siren first.

"Here's the police!" he yelped, louder than any of them.

They fell silent.

Car doors slammed outside.

Tara Snow lurched to her feet, drenched and filthy yet vicious with triumph. "I told you I'd called the police," she taunted them, and began to snigger. "Wait till they see that animal. And this water. Do you realize how much it will cost to pump it out and put everything in order? It's not hygienic. You'll have rot and raw sewage to contend with. You'll never be able to afford to open again. You'll still have to close down. And I'll force a protection order on some of those clocks and instruments, and then —"

"You won't," Ben bawled at her. "You're not having any of it." He glanced at Mom, expecting her to agree, but was startled by the heartbroken expression on her face. *Why does she look like that?* he thought. *Surely once the workers come and pump all the water away, everything will be all right again?*

Tara Snow continued to rant.

Ben turned to the hippo. "She's talking nonsense, isn't she?" he begged. "You said everything was under control."

The hippo's sodden hide looked a shade darker from the water. He gazed at Ben wearily.

Ben persisted: "You can get rid of this water on your own. I know you can. The water outside didn't harm you. You've got the diamond. Use it. Blow the water away like you did before."

Listlessly the hippo sighed. "The diamond is nighttime magic," he said. "I feel its weakness as the sun rises. And there are people coming. I don't feel in control. I can't blow — I feel all puffed out. You must tell me what to do, as I can't think clearly anymore."

"Don't let us down now!" Ben cried. His fists were clenched so tightly that he felt like his knuckles would pop from their joints. "Just try. It's early — the sun's not very high yet. There must be something you can do to get rid of this water. Something big. I don't care how you do it. If you can't blow . . . I don't know . . . drink it up if you have to."

He didn't literally mean drink.

Nevertheless, the hippo dropped his head and began to lap up the water.

And What He Drank

CHAPTER 42

Concentric ripples spread as the hippo gulped.

"That wasn't what I meant," Ben wailed. "I meant *do something magic.*"

Yet when he tried to explain what that could be, the words tangled around his tongue and all he could do was stutter with frustration while the hippo continued to gulp and the ripples spread, ring within ring within ring.

Ben began to feel as if he were in the desperate sort of dream where you call for help but you can't make anyone understand. He felt exhausted, heavy with failure; he wondered how he had ever thought he could save the museum from a flooding river.

Would Dad have been proud that he had tried — even though he hadn't succeeded? He didn't know. And lost in his own defeated gaze, he watched the ripples multiply and hypnotically shift across the pool. Gradually the electric tension left his limbs, and he fancied that the ripples pulsed with his own heartbeat, ring inside ring inside ring, while he was caught in a trance, caught out of time.

No one else moved or said anything either, but in this sudden dreamlike state, that didn't seem strange to Ben. Neither did the odd impression that the ripples were changing. He knew this had to be an illusion, but it certainly appeared that the circles in the water now undulated toward the hippo and had begun to rotate. And there was music too — the "Aquarium" music he'd heard when he'd first come into the museum — and his stone-dry eyes seemed to watch through a whirling gauze until all the particles that made up the room became visible, swirling and shimmering and separating.

Only the hippo remained solid in the center of this spinning vortex. Occasionally, though, Ben thought he glimpsed a face: at one point, Mom seemed close, wearing her most quizzical expression, then she was gone and Constance swept by, upright and serene; the kangaroos bounced briefly past, followed by the giraffes, and then a merry-go-round procession of camels and zebras and bears and birds, with the collared peccaries trotting to keep up. Flummery fluttered among them with the sengi and Leon perched on his back, present for a moment, then gone, as the spinning increased until everything blurred. And then Ben thought he saw the Garner-Gee family from the portrait in the hall, and Dad was with them too, but as he groped to see more, this most fleeting vision was sucked away with all the rest, like water down a drain.

All at once there was a rupture in the dimness, a tiny rip with frayed edges, a split in the center of his bleary thoughts that grew as if someone tugged at the fabric of the dream, and then entirely ripped it apart, when a man's voice, commanding and edgy, called, "Police. Anyone here?"

After a moment a policewoman added, "Well, someone must be here — who do you think opened the door?"

A third replied, "Beats me. There isn't a soul around — apart from the birds and the bees." This last man giggled at his own bad joke, though the laughter sounded forced. Ben guessed that this third police officer was scared.

"The door must have been left unlocked," declared the policewoman's voice.

It wasn't, thought Ben. *Leon must have opened it.*

The voices had an odd cupped sound because they were issuing from the room's speaker. Blinking and bemused, he stared at the speaker, realizing vaguely that someone must have stepped on the trip button in the lobby. He was surprised that the thing still worked underwater.

Then, like a slap in the face, he realized that there was no water.

Wide awake, he gazed at the atrium.

The flood had vanished!

All the large animals were back on their plinths: the panther and the lioness and the giraffes that flanked the stairs, the kangaroo and the ostrich and the polar bear, and the armadillo and the rest — all of them poised as they had been the day before and all the days before that. It was as if nothing had ever moved. None of them looked even damp, or at all the worse for the night's adventure; neither did the smaller exhibits, which were all safely behind the glass doors of their cabinets.

Yet something was different. The old dinginess was missing. The museum appeared brighter: paintwork fresh and clean, cracks in the plaster healed. All that remained of the flood was a damp sheen on the floor, as if someone had been overzealous with a mop.

Through the speaker, he could hear the police talking among themselves.

"My, aren't they lucky?" the "in-charge" voice said. "Water lapping at the walls outside, yet still bone-dry in here. When did the flood engineers say they'd be over?"

"Later this morning, with the water pumps."

"Good. They'll have a mess outside to sort out, but it looks like they might be OK in here."

"What a miracle. It's a fabulous place. Imagine if —"

"Anyone there?" the policewoman called out. Then she said to her colleagues, "Maybe you're wrong about the owner living here. Seems an odd place to live —"

"An amazing place to live," said the younger policeman, and Ben saw Constance smile. He noticed, not for the first time, that her smile was exactly like that of the girl in the painting.

"Ben," she called, "would you nip out and greet our guests? I feel a little slow and stiff this morning."

Ben grinned back, and he would indeed have nipped, if Tara Snow hadn't struggled to her feet and shoved him sharply against the wall.

"They're *my* police," she said, leering with deadened eyes, breathing stale grown-up morning breath in his face. "I called them."

Ben's voice came out in a squeak: "You can't own the police."

"Stay away from my son," Mom yelled. She was hobbling toward them. "Come away from her, Ben."

The police must have heard Mom shouting, because abruptly the hallway rang with running boots. One at a time, they issued from the hallway: first came a pepper-haired man — the one with the "in-charge" voice — slightly pink as if he didn't often move beyond a walk. Close behind him came the policewoman. She looked kind and a bit worn out around the eyes, like Mom. At the rear came a younger policeman who had short curly hair and a dazed expression. He stopped in the entrance and gawped in delight.

"Wow!" he said, gazing at the atrium — whereupon Tara Snow let go of Ben and threw herself at him so that he almost lost his balance. She clung to his sleeve, jabbing her finger viciously at the hippo, muttering accusations, and her voice rose higher and higher until everyone heard her wail, "And then it ate my phone!"

There was a silence.

"Ate?" said the older policeman with a crooked smile. He strode down the courtyard steps and delivered a slap to the hippo's flank. The sound rang hollow. The hippo rocked woodenly as the policeman turned and shrugged. "Doesn't seem very dangerous to me."

Constance coughed. "A little care, officer," she called mildly. "That was my grandfather's favorite exhibit, and I am very fond of it. He brought it here in 1892."

The policeman pulled his hands away as though he'd been caught stealing. "I'm terribly sorry," he said. "Don't know what came over me. It's been a long night, and —"

"Quite," said Constance, striding toward him, holding out her hand like a queen.

The policewoman took Tara Snow's elbow and gently tried to steer her away. "You don't look very well, love. I think you may have had a fall and hurt your head. Why don't we go and sit in my car and you can tell me everything?"

Tara Snow didn't want to be comforted; spittle gathered at the corners of her mouth as she protested hysterically, "Don't you dare patronize me! You're not listening. See that old woman there? She's abducted my colleague, Mr. Pike, and then I think that hippo ate him."

"He did not!" Ben shouted.

Everyone turned toward Ben. It appeared that the police hadn't noticed him before. Now the young policeman strode over to him. "What's your name, son? What are you doing here?"

"Yes, you should question that boy," ranted Tara Snow, clinging to the older policeman now. "He's a trespasser. I found him up to all sorts of mischief outside — on his own in the middle of the night. I think he did all this."

"Did what?" said Constance, gesturing at the museum.

"And I'm not on my own," said Ben.

"He's with me," said Mom, limping forward. "I'm his mother."

"Mom's hurt her ankle," added Ben, hurrying to support her with one arm around her waist.

"It's quite true," said Constance, who had crossed the courtyard surprisingly swiftly. "And he certainly is not trespassing. He is my cousin and my heir, so has every right to be here. I'm afraid the lady over there is the intruder — though let's be kind — I think perhaps she's not feeling quite well."

The room erupted then. Indignant protests from Tara Snow combined with the steady voices of the police and Constance's firm assurances. Ben surprised himself by feeling abruptly tearful and shaky, but Mom was there, hugging him and smiling, rubbing his shoulders as she whispered, "Don't worry, my love. It was a terrible, wonderful night, but it'll be all right now. Oh, I'm so proud of you, Ben. Everyone's so proud of you."

And as he looked into her eyes, he knew exactly who she meant.

Eventually the two older officers guided Tara Snow away, though from the atrium, they could hear her objecting all along the hall. The younger policeman remained to make a report. Actually he looked rather pleased to be allowed to stay. He gazed around almost rapturously. And certainly the museum looked truly beautiful as the early winter sunlight dusted all the fur and feathers with amber, and bathed the woodwork and metalwork in morning tangerine gold.

Constance sighed deeply. "It's been a long night for us," she said wearily. "Would you mind, officer? I think we'd all be more comfortable upstairs."

So the policeman helped Mom up the steps on one side, and Ben helped her on the other — or maybe she helped Ben; it was hard to say. And soon enough they were warming themselves by the fire, drinking tea and eating a delicious breakfast of toast and honey, and Ben felt snug and yawny.

"What an amazing place," the policeman kept repeating. "I never knew about it. I can't wait to bring my kids."

"Oh, you must bring them," said Constance, exchanging a look with Mom. "You'd be most welcome. I have an idea we'll be open more often in the future."

The policeman told them he thought there ought to be compensation from the city for the flooding of the grounds. "They should have kept that weir in better shape," he said. "There's flood funds for this sort of thing. They'll have insurance."

And Mom agreed that she thought there would be some sort of grant they could apply for now.

Thus it was that they descended into dull grown-up conversation, so after Ben had noted that the pufferfish and the Little Ship of Venice were back in their usual places, he snuggled into the worn softness of the sofa.

He perked up briefly when he heard the policeman mention museum shops, and what a good idea they were, and how visitors liked to spend money in them. Mom was smiling and saying how she'd like a change, while Constance was looking delighted too. Ben had one of his ideas then, but he caught the eye of the pufferfish, who winked, and Ben reflected that it might be best to let the grown-ups think all the good ideas were theirs, because then they'd be more likely to act upon them. Besides, his head was sinking into a green velvet cushion, and very cozy it was against his cheek while the fire crackled and warmed. He wanted to hear some more about museum shops, but his eyes kept rolling back behind his lids.

The last thing he was aware of was the sengi's voice in his ear: "We always told you everything was under control," she whispered. "The family only needed to work together again, and you made them do it, Ben."

But before he could ask her what she meant, he was asleep.

OPENING TIME

IN JUNE THAT YEAR, CONSTANCE GARNER-GEE HOSTED A reception for Friends of the Gee Museum. Lots of invitations were sent out.

This is how they looked:

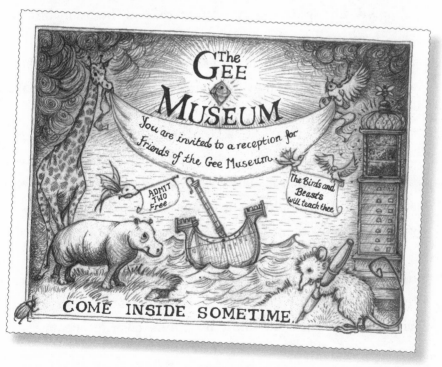

The GEE MUSEUM

You are invited to a reception for Friends of the Gee Museum

ADMIT TWO Free

The Birds and Beasts will teach thee

COME INSIDE SOMETIME.

This time there was an address on the back of the invitation. Also included were the new extended opening hours, in case anyone couldn't attend or wanted to come a second time or many times, which, as it turned out, everybody did.

Ben and his mother did not need an invitation. They had already moved permanently to the Gee Museum and now lived in an attic apartment that had lain empty since Montgomery Garner-Gee had vacated it.

It was true that they had found a century's worth of cobwebs and dust up there, but once they had cleaned it up — and rehoused the spiders, and a giant case of hummingbirds, and three models of a Senegalese house, and an elaborate mechanical swan — they made a home that was full of sunlight and history. It was much roomier and cozier than their basement apartment had ever been. And much more fun.

The weather that June was perfect — rainy, windy, and damp — which meant that all the picnics and sports games had been canceled, so that absolutely everyone came to the reception at the Gee Museum. Even the mayor and the city councillors were there, eager to make amends for the flood damage.

The younger policeman brought his family and also some friends who were off duty and liked museums, and some teachers from Ben's school were there too, and lots of his friends with their parents, and most of Mom's favorite customers from the old shop. They said they would recommend it to everyone — especially as the new Discovery Museum had unexplainably closed until further notice. No one quite knew why, although (and here they lowered their voices) they had heard the director — a certain Miss Snow — had taken time off work: due to nerves, so someone had said. In fact, it was generally assumed that she had gone away until further notice and was unlikely to continue in her present post.

On the day of the reception, the front door of the museum seemed to open and close almost magically without anyone touching it. Inside, Constance Garner-Gee greeted her guests, standing in the lobby in a new blue dress that made her look as elegant as a slightly toppling delphinium.

"Marvelous for her age," the grown-ups said, smiling, and a few wondered, *How old can she be?* For surely she had seen more than a lifetime of openings and closings.

However, no one dreamed of asking, for that would have been impolite, and Constance Garner-Gee certainly wasn't telling (and neither were the bees). She simply smiled with a smile exactly like the girl in the painting behind her and invited her guests to wander as they chose.

Beside her on the counter was a small silver dial in the shape of a ship, and down from its perch, for the party, was a scops owl. It was stuffed, of course, but children were invited to touch — if they were gentle — and on that day they all wanted to stroke and be gentle, though only until they discovered that the room next door (which used to be the egg room) now contained a lovely new museum shop.

It should be mentioned that the young policeman was correct: the shop that Mom opened in the Gee Museum was a huge success. There was plenty of room for everything she liked to sell, and now she could stock more interesting books and craft materials, including cut-out-and-color moving paper kits modeled on the museum clocks. There were also beeswax candles, along with all the usual gifts you find in a museum shop: postcards, and erasers in the shape of salamanders, and beetle fridge magnets of several varieties, and pencils topped with plastic frogs, and peacock-feather pens. The children especially admired the huge selection of cuddly toys, including a furry chameleon and a striped bee hand puppet. Ben's personal favorite was a chocolate bar with a picture of the hippo drawn in white icing. Mom sold a great many of these, though she swore that it was partly thanks to the stuffed elephant shrew, which had a new position right near the cash register. She said it glared so hard at customers that they rarely dared to leave without buying at least a bar of chocolate.

That evening, though, even the shop didn't hold anyone for long because they had all been told that Honeybun Tearooms was providing refreshments in the atrium. Most people headed straight there, though a few ventured into the insect room and might have noticed that the crystal hive was sparkling clean and buzzing with life.

Nobody bothered with the bottle room, where the silver bottle lay, safely locked away in the table cabinet behind the door. It was a stuffy, dark room and no one liked going in there much. Perhaps one day, when Constance had decided what to do about it, they would open the table cabinet up — but that wouldn't be in the near future.

The near future was for happy times, Ben thought, as he ate chocolate cake with cherries on top until he felt so full he had to change to honey cake. He looked at the hippo smiling his eternal smile and wondered what he was thinking. It was hard to tell because those glass eyes were always open.

The truth was, now that all was well at the Gee Museum, the hippo, who had been keeping watch for such a very long time, was fast asleep.

Author's Note

Eleven years ago, at the other end of a long hallway in the Harvard Museum of Natural History, I saw a stuffed pygmy hippopotamus. I sketched it, because I like sketching in museums and because it seemed important. As I drew, I had a sense of waiting for something to happen, waiting for someone to arrive, waiting not only in the present but in the past and the future simultaneously, and it seemed, just then, that the hippo was waiting in all of those times too. Perhaps it was waiting for me to write this book.

I love museums. It seems to me that in every museum there are some exhibits (like that hippo) that appear to have more life about them than the rest. Often these objects have been much handled, so they can appear worn and grimy, or else they are shiny with use, or polish. Perhaps they were especially treasured for a while, or the person who found them had been seeking them for a long time, or the craftsperson who created them loved them so much he or she didn't want to part with them. Indeed, it is almost as if they are haunted by the thoughts and fingerprints of the people who once loved them.

Why do humans collect things? So many of us do. Is our yearning to choose, and own, and arrange, one of the ways we try to control our chaotic lives? Perhaps we even collect and order things to distract ourselves from the slip and slide of time. I am a collector myself. I have collected the characters for my book from real museums I have visited. I have sifted and shifted my collection until it formed a story in my own imaginary museum: the Gee Museum.

I also collected two real folktales and retold them within the story. The watercow story is a folktale from Liberia. The egg-witch story originates in eastern Europe. And I like to entwine my words with extra visual stories, so I hope readers will enjoy visiting the Gee Museum in the illustrations too. I've made many drawings of it now. They are based on my sketches in the museums I have visited in the last ten years. I owe a particular debt to the Harvard Museum of Natural History, in Cambridge, Massachusetts where I first saw the hippo, and also the glass apple, and the elephant bird's egg. Flummery and the sitting polar bear come from the Natural History Museum at Tring, just outside London. And a special mention must go to Oxford, where I live: the sengi, the live bees, the witch in the bottle, the Little Ship of Venice, and too many others to mention were inspired by exhibits in the Oxford University museums — indeed, some of the story was written in the Natural History Museum café.

The museums I have mentioned thus far are wonderful scientific institutions. However, I think the Gee Museum itself is more like the small museums that you can find in most towns, the sort of museums that are sometimes in danger of closure because people have forgotten about them or never really looked hard at them, the sort of museums that have a more eclectic collection and were often founded by generous people who dreamed of sharing their private passion with other people in the future. Sometimes in those places, when I listen hard in the shadows, I think I can almost catch their words and thoughts gathering in layers together with the thoughts and words of past visitors. And I wonder if what we call the atmosphere of a building is actually a certain kind of alchemy made up of these leftover moments.

Finally, thanks also to the friends and family and editors who read the story before publication and advised and encouraged me, especially Pandora Dewan, Hilary Delamere, Rebecca Gowers, David Fickling, and Annie Eaton. Thank you so much — this book would not be the same without you.